The Slurpee Chronicles:
Giving You the Tea

K.D. WILSON

ISBN: 1469976900
ISBN 13: 9781469976907

The Slurpee Chronicles:
Giving You the Tea

Chapter 1

"Hello?"

I didn't recognize the number on my caller ID, but as soon as I heard that sexy, deep, manly voice on the other end, I knew exactly who it was.

"Say my nigga, wassup? What you doin' right now?"

"Nothin' major, I'm just watchin' TV."

"Well shit come over here and hook me up."

"I'm on my way."

Every time I hear Mike's voice my mouth instantly gets moist. I already know what he wants. He wants me to come over there and suck his big, fat, long, milk chocolaty ass dick! Mike is the first nigga I ever sucked in my life, and I practically owe him for introducing me to the world of dick sucking. Anytime Mike calls me I will drop whatever I'm doing to satisfy him in a way that only I can. Oh by the way, Mike just so happens to be my cousin. Now hold up and let me explain before you start thinking I'm one of them nasty ass, triflin', dick suckin' bitches on TV or something. He aint even my real cousin. He's a friend of the family and we just call ourselves cousins. I'm sixteen and he's twenty years old. We not even blood related at all. Well hell, let me let you in on how we even started fucking around in the first place.

My name is La'Darious Moss, but everybody calls me LD. I have lived in Dallas, Texas my whole life. We are currently living in a ghetto, raggedy ass Section 8 apartment complex. Everyone calls our apartments *The Purps*. The owner painted them some ugly ass shade of purple and that's how the name came about. This is what you would actually call *the hood*. Most of the people living over here are either low or no income families. Some of the apartments here are really overcrowded and have like ten people living inside a single three-bedroom unit. There is hardly ever a dull moment over here either; there is always some shit going down.

Only three of my momma's six kids are living with us right now. It's four people total living in our apartment: Bernadine, my mother; Damonte, my brother who is five; Sasha, my sister who is four; and myself. I have never met my mother's oldest three kids, which also happens to be two boys and a girl. I don't even know what their names are because my mother rarely even mentions them. About a year before I was born, Child Protective Services took the oldest three kids away because my momma would leave them home alone at all hours of the night. From what I've gathered, through listening to my aunts and uncles talk, is that she was out turning tricks for cash. The only time she even mentions the incident is when she is talking about how *that white bitch* at CPS was trying to set her up. Yea I already know what you're thinking; I thought the same thing when I heard her say that ignorant ass shit for the first time too-*This bitch has got to be crazy*! Clearly my mom was the one setting her self up for failure by leaving a five, three, and one year old home alone. This bitch also said that she was not about to give up her Section 8 and food stamps so that's how I came along; she had to have another kid before it was time for her to go recertify her Section 8. This hoe got pregnant with me cause she didn't want to lose her fucking government assistance-*Really bitch?*

I rarely get to see my younger brother and sister. Ever since my momma started getting her government funded childcare assistance, she has constantly kept them in daycare. They practically live at the daycare facility. She even found a 24-hour facility that will accept them any time she wants to drop them off. She told the owner some story about her working two jobs and not being able to be there with them like she needs to. I think she may have fucked that old white man too! The government only pays him for forty hour's worth of childcare each week, and I know damn well he aint gone have his crew watch them two bad ass kids just for the hell of it. They would go out of business if every bitch in the ghetto went to him with they story as to why they can't watch they own fucking kids. My mother obviously has a gift, she can con anyone into doing exactly what she wants them to do without them ever realizing that she has just manipulated the system for the millionth time. If only she put as much time and effort into finding employment, we would surely be moving out of the hood in no time.

The majority of the kids in my apartments come from single parent households that lack any kind of structure or guidance. Our mothers frequently have casual sex and get pregnant by these low life niggas that don't want anything to do with them or us. All these niggas around here want is a quick fuck, and someone to take care of them financially. They tell these naive women anything they want to hear just to have sex with them, and then they run off and leave they dumb asses for the next dumb bitch that's willing to let them lay up for free. Now don't get me wrong, I'm thankful to both of my parents for my gift of life, but I also wish I had at least one sane parent that would have made the ultimate sacrifice of taking the time to raise me properly.

As far as my dad goes, I have nothing good at all to say about him. I only remember two interactions with that hoe ass nigga throughout my life. The last one was when I was six years old. I asked him for some new shoes for Christmas. He told me OK, and he said that he would be right back with them. It's ten years later, and I'm still waiting on that nigga to come back with my damn shoes. Clearly my mother makes terrible choices in men. Matter of fact, I don't even think she has a damn clue who the daddies of the youngest two are!

From pictures that I have seen, my mother used to be real fine back in her day. She was really pretty, skinny, had a fat ass, slim waist, and didn't mind letting any nigga get a taste-*for the right price*. She is about five-foot-six, light skinned, and has short black hair. However, she wears weave to make it much more longer than it really is. People always ask her if she's mixed. She constantly lies and tells them she is mixed with Indian. I can't wait for the day when someone asks her ass what kind of Indian she's mixed with. I know the only reply she'll be able to have is, "Indian Remy, eighteen inch, 1B!"

Over the years she has really let herself go. She currently weighs about two hundred and fifty pounds. What puzzles me is that as fat as she is, she has never had a problem finding a man. My mother always got some random nigga staying here with us, but please don't let Section 8 hear about that shit. This bitch will have a fit if they were to find out she got a nigga living in here rent-free. Every time Section 8 comes to do an inspection at our apartment, she'll have whatever nigga is staying with us at the time haul all his shit out of here so motherfucking fast, you would think he was an illegal Mexican and immigration was coming through to pick his ass up. She does this so the inspector won't suspect someone is living here that's not on her lease.

As soon as the inspector leaves, the niggas haul all they shit right back in here.

My momma is one of those old bitter bitches that can't stand anyone. She doesn't have any female friends cause she says they all hate on her. I honestly think it's because she has a reputation of fucking all of her friend's niggas. Anytime she is fighting with someone it's over a dusty ass nigga, or she claims that some hoe is jealous of her. I'm not sure what it is that she has, or why in the hell she would think anyone is jealous of her, cause she don't have shit! Now mind you, she is on every government aid they ever came up with. She gets Section 8, Food stamps, WIC, Childcare, Disability, and Medicaid! Don't even ask me how the fuck she does it, because I aint never seen nobody get as much assistance from the government as this hoe get and always talking bout she aint got no damn money.

My momma used to be on drugs real bad too. Damn, I sat up here and said *used to* like this bitch has miraculously turned over a new leaf or something. You know how the saying goes, "Once a fiend, always a fiend." Her ass still be out here trickin' for cash and snorting that bullshit right up her nose. She try to put on a front for us like she don't do cocaine anymore, but I absolutely refuse to believe that bullshit. You can actually tell when she on the shit too. She'll come out of her room with a surprised ass look in her eyes; the biggest fucking set of eyes you ever did see. You would think that hoe just won the damn lottery or something.

She is always sniffing like her damn nose is constantly running. Whenever anyone says something to her about all that damn sniffing she says, "Oh excuse me, I got a head cold." This bitch has had this same head cold for about a year now. I am not an ear, nose, and throat specialist by any means, but I have never in my life heard of a fucking head cold lasting that damn long! With as much aid as this hoe gets, surely she could have gotten her so-called *head cold* fixed by now.

She also walks around here everyday singing to herself, or to anyone that will pay her any attention. Her favorite verse to sing is, "Cause I'm a bad bitch." She places so much emphasis on those words that you would think she is trying to convince everyone in the nation that those words are actually true. In my head all I can think to myself is, *No sweetie, you're a bad built bitch!* However, I just shake my head and keep my thoughts to myself.

Chapter 2

I don't have any excuses or no bullshit ass sob stories for you about being molested by some old ass man, or even being raped and shit when I was younger. I like dick simply because…I like dick. Any sexual act that I have ever engaged in has been consensual. Honestly, I have always wanted to suck dick for as long as I can remember. Shit I knew I was gay from birth. My momma should have known too. Out of all six of her kids, I was the only one she had to have a C-section with. She said I was stubborn and didn't want to come out. I sat my gay ass in her stomach and wouldn't budge. I knew there had to be an alternate route I could take out of there. I may have only been a infant, but even then there was no way in hell you were getting me to bust through anyone's pussy! I was also the only one she couldn't breast feed. She said something about me not being able to "latch on" to her titties. Well hell, she should see the way I *latch on* to these niggas dicks now. She would be so proud!

I started sucking dick when I was twelve, and I must say that I have enjoyed my last four years of faithful service. I secretly go by the name "Slurpee." Around our hood Slurpee is famous for sucking all the thugs dicks. However, none of them will admit that they have actually fucked with me if you were to ask them. Hell, I will even deny it myself. I keep my business on the low. They know that all they have to ask me to do is *hook them up*, and I will drop to my knees wherever and whenever to drain every drop of nut out of them.

I think I have mastered the art of dick sucking, and I don't play around while I'm sucking dick. I don't sit there and peck at it like a fuckin' chicken, or lick on it like a lollipop. I get down and dirty with it. They come to me cause they want the best, and I make damn sure I give it to them every time. I don't waist any time pullin' they meat out to start suckin' on it either. I know my role, and I understand that they have to get back home to their wives, girlfriends, or baby mommas before they dumb asses ever knew what happened. I don't really give a fuck about them having women in their lives either. They obviously aint doing they jobs if they nigga sticking his dick in my mouth. I'm not trying to take none of them from they hoes either. Shit, I'm the one keeping them together if you ask me! One thing these hoes need to realize is that we all gotta' share. They teach us in kindergarten that sharing is caring.

They can think they man faithful all they want, but trust me they gone share him. Whether it's voluntarily or involuntarily is on them.

Honestly, its just casual sex between us. There is no emotional attachment to these niggas what so ever. I don't try to get to know them at all. I don't care about how they day went, or what's going on in their confused ass lives. I don't give a fuck if they grandma got run over by a fucking reindeer last night! Just shut the fuck up and stick that dick in my mouth so I can drain them nuts and leave! Just a real blow and motherfucking go.

All the niggas around here know they can come to me for some good ass head, and I won't run my mouth like all them other gossiping ass punks in our hood. Punks, queens, sissies, fags, and homos are all terms people in my projects use to refer to homosexual men. I never have been one to hang around a bunch of punks, because the ones around here are way too messy for me. All them queens like to do is just sit around and cackle like some bitch ass hens! All you hear is a bunch of "Chile, Girl, Bitch, and Trust", along with lip smacking, and finger snapping all throughout they conversations. I wouldn't say that I'm above the average punk, but I have never really identified with them as much.

Growing up I never really acted gay like them other queens, but I don't act all thuggish either. I did all the things any normal boy would do. I rode my bike around the neighborhood with all my homeboys, and I played little league football. I secretly wanted to be on the sidelines as a cheerleader though, but I knew early on that would be committing suicide for my reputation. I can remember times I would sit in my room and dream of being a cheerleader and would run through every cheer I had learned. I would go to football practice and secretly despise all them little fast ass hoes kicking and screaming from the sidelines and cheering us on. Hell I knew all of the cheers they performed and could do them way better than most of them ratchet ass hoes could. I just couldn't come to terms with being a fag in public and doing all that girly shit around my hood. I knew my people wouldn't approve of that shit, and I didn't want to feel like the black sheep.

I have never been a big guy. I'm sixteen; I stand about five-foot-four, and weigh around one hundred and ten pounds. I'm pretty petite and most people accuse me of being a pretty boy. I mostly hang around nothing but straight guys. I have sucked the majority of them up though. Ironically, they still identify themselves as straight, even though they are constantly sticking they dicks in my mouth. I'm probably the one to blame for them thinking that shit too. I always talk they dumbasses into giving up the dick. I tell them that they not gay if they let another nigga suck them up. I also tell them shit like, "A mouth is a mouth", or "It aint gay if you're the one getting your dick sucked." They stupid asses actually believe that dumb shit too. But hey, what ever gets them to sleep at night. They can think they still straight all day long. As long as I can get the dick, I'm fine with that.

Chapter 3

I was twelve years old when we first moved to The Purps. My mom moved here because we had family that lived over here and they were able to get her broke ass a hook up on the security deposit. Because of my light skin color, I had to fight from day one just to prove myself to the niggas that already lived over here. For some reason niggas in the hood always want to fight on the light skinned people cause they see you as weak. Most of the time it was a one on one fight. My cousin Mike, who was sixteen at the time and his two brothers; AJ, who was nineteen; and Boo, who was twelve; would always have my back if anyone tried to jump in. AJ, Mike, and Boo weren't really my cousins in all actuality. My uncle dated their mom for a while so we kind of grew up together. We considered ourselves cousins even after they broke up, despite us not being blood related at all.

Boo and I were the same age and played football together on the neighborhood little league team. I was the starting running back and he was the starting wide receiver. We would hang out together all the time and we were known as the stars of our team. We made the most touchdowns during the games and everyone said we both would have a future in the NFL. They pretty much filled Boo's head up with all that dumb shit. I did have dreams of being rich and living in a big house one day, but I knew my gay ass wasn't going to the fucking NFL. Every nigga in the hood seemed to have the same dreams: to be a rapper, or in the NBA, or in the NFL. What the fuck happened to the aspiring lawyers, doctors, or any profession that you have to receive an education for? I knew there wasn't a future in sports for me. I had my mind (and pretty soon my mouth) on all the players; my heart wasn't in the game at all. Hell, the only reason I even played football was to be next to all them sexy ass niggas from our hood. I was attracted to them all, but no one knew that besides me. I would sneak a peek at their bodies every time we changed in and out of our gear. At first I felt really weird about doing that gay shit. I quickly learned how to handle those feelings though.

~ ~ ~ ~

I was over Boo's house after football practice one summer. Their mother was never home just like mine wasn't. They pretty much did whatever they wanted to do. AJ was Boo's older brother, and he didn't seem to like me very much. He had my back in the streets, but he would always try to embarrass me and make remarks saying that I was soft or gay. I never understood why he had so much hatred toward me, and I was glad he wasn't there while me and Boo played video games. It was always awkward being in the same room with him for too long.

It was about two in the morning and Boo had fallen asleep. I was still up playing video games when I heard Mike come through the door.

"Wassup LD?"

Mike smelled like he had just got through smoking a pound of weed. His crew that he hung with was known for being the neighborhood drug dealers. Well I wouldn't actually call them drug dealers. It wasn't like they broke asses was moving some major work. To me, it seemed as though they smoked way more weed than they actually sold. They were just some ol' nickel and dime ass niggas that had our projects on lock. The apartment that Mike and his crew sold drugs out of was known as, "The Trap." It was the spot where everyone in our apartments went to buy their drugs from. Mike was only sixteen, but he had a body that was built like a grown ass man. He looked so motherfucking good wearing his white muscle shirt and black basketball shorts hanging off his ass. He was taller than me, he was muscular, and he had a dark chocolate complexion. He had pretty white teeth and all the neighborhood girls wanted to, or had already fucked him.

"Nothin', just playing this game."

"Where everybody else at?"

"AJ not here, and Boo sleep. Where you comin' from?"

"I was at the trap, then I went to Keisha house. I was tryna' fuck, but she was trippin' and shit. Talkin' bout I'm gone think she a hoe if she let me fuck. Man I told that hoe to get the fuck on with all that bullshit. She done got me horny as hell for nothing."

I looked over at Mike, he was still standing the whole time we were talking. I saw him grabbing his dick through his basketball shorts. I was in a daze for a while, well more like under a spell. I was fixated on that big ass bulge that was in his shorts. I had never seen anything like it. I stared at it for what seemed like an eternity. The sound of my character dying on the television had to snap me back into reality. I looked up at Mike's face and he just smiled.

"I'm bout to go to sleep LD, I'll holla at ya."

I sat there in front of the TV and I felt weird. There I was, looking at Mike with his big hard dick staring me in my face, and I couldn't turn away from it. The thought of Mike's dick made me get on hard myself. I didn't know what to make of all that. I knew I liked guys, but I had never acted on my impulse. I wouldn't even know the first thing to do if the opportunity even presented itself. Just as all those thoughts were running through my head, Mike called me into his room.

I walked into Mike's room and he said, "Lock my door and sit down on the bed."

Mike was lying in the bed, under his covers, with his shirt off. I looked at the TV and I saw two naked guys, and a girl was performing oral sex on both of them. Mike was watching a fucking porno! All I could think was, *why did he call me in here*?

Mike pulled his covers off of him, and to my surprise he was just lying there in the bed butt ass naked! He was stroking the longest, and fattest black dick I had ever seen. I was nervous at this point. I had never seen a dick so fucking huge! It was strange to me because I felt nervous and excited at the same time. I instantly got rock hard just looking at Mike's dick. I tried to look away but I just couldn't.

"I saw you staring at it, I thought you wanted to see what it look like."

I snapped at him, "I wasn't staring at yo' dick nigga." Clearly I was a brand new punk and needed proper training, because I didn't even know how to respond to him.

Mike just chuckled as he said, "Yes you was bro. Come touch it, if you aint all scared and shit."

I rolled my eyes at him, "I'm not scared!"

Actually I was! I was shaking on the inside, but I didn't let him know that.

"Well come stroke it for me."

Mike just lay there stroking his dick with the sexiest smile on his face. All kinds of thoughts began to race through my head. *What if this was a set up? What if he was just trying to see if I was one of them undercover faggots AJ had always accused me of being and then tell everyone in the neighborhood about me?* I don't know what came over me at that point but I couldn't resist any longer. I just had to touch it. I sat on the bed and reached my hand out to touch Mike's dick. I started stroking it and he just moaned as I held his big ass dick in my hand. I went up and down on it for about a minute, and then he told me to put it in my mouth. I was prepared to do whatever Mike wanted me to do. I didn't know the first thing about sucking dick, but if that's what Mike's sexy ass wanted, I was going to give it to him.

He stood up and I got on my knees in front of him. I grabbed his dick and I put it in my mouth. It was so fat that it barely even fit. I just had the head of it resting inside my mouth. It felt kind of weird to me. It felt like a big ass stick of meat just sitting inside my mouth. He told me to suck on it, so I did. He continued to coach me throughout the whole ordeal.

"Suck on it like a popsicle."

His dick was so big that I couldn't even respond. Everything that came out was sort of a muffled sound. I must have been doing it just like he wanted, because he moaned loudly as he began to thrust his dick in and out of my mouth. His dick suddenly got rock hard, and it had swollen up even fatter than it already was! It wasn't long before he started pissing in my mouth! I started gagging and spit out some creamy, white, salty shit on his floor.

"Nigga u pissed in my mouth?"

Mike just laughed, "Naw my nigga, I nutted in yo' mouth."

"Why the fuck did you do that?"

Mike just grinned and said, "That's what I'm suppose to do. You should have swallowed all of it too."

All I could say was, "Oh."

I was so embarrassed. How could I be so fucking dumb as to think Mike would piss in my mouth? I should have known that he was going to nut. This was my first time doing anything sexual; so I was very inexperienced-to say the least. Mike didn't seem to mind at all. He just sat down on the bed smiling at me and shaking his head. He seemed to be so relaxed after busting his 1st nut in my mouth.

Just as soon as Mike's smile came across his face, it went away. He had a look of anger in his eyes. He looked at me and said, "You better keep this between us my nigga; nobody bet' not find out about this shit!" I was confused at this point. I didn't know if Mike was threatening me to scare me into silence, or if he was actually scared himself. Honestly, I think it was a little of both.

"Man I aint gon' tell nobody about this shit, you don't even have to worry about that!"

"Alright LD, I'm just makin' sure. That head was real good, but I don't want anyone thinkin' I'm a faggot and shit."

"Yea it's all good bro. I definitely don't want nobody thinkin' I'm one either."

From that point on, I knew that whatever happened between Mike and I would stay between us. Hell if I did tell anyone, who would really believe me? Mike didn't act, look, or possess any gay tendencies. As many hoes as Mike had on his team, I would have a better chance of getting people to believe in the fucking Loch Ness Monster, than to believe that I had actually sucked his dick. I wouldn't dare tell anyone either way. I adopted my "privacy act" from that point forward. I wasn't going to be the type to suck and tell. I wanted Mike to be confident that anytime his dick needed to get away for a while, it would find a safe haven inside my mouth.

Mike just stood up and smiled at me again. He was wiping his dick off with a towel he had on the bed. He thanked me for the head as he walked to the bathroom. He was still completely naked, and watching him walk away turned me on even more. His body was so dark and muscular. Just the sight of his naked ass made me want his dick in my mouth one more time. This was when I realized that I loved sucking dick. Being able to please a man with my oral abilities turned me on more than I had ever known. To give Mike so much satisfaction that he moaned in ecstasy and poured his unborn kids into my mouth was enough to drive me insane. I was on a mission to become the best dick sucker this side of the Mississippi River. I needed proper training though. I knew I didn't do a great job the first time, and I had to get better. I took Mike's DVD out of the player and took it with me. Fuck playing the game at their house, I was going to go home and watch his porno over and over, until I mastered the art of dick sucking. Next time Mike wants his dick sucked I was going to show *him* a thing or two!

Chapter 4

It had been about a week since I had my first dick sucking experience with Mike. I had seen him everyday since then and we interacted normally with each other. It wasn't awkward or anything between us. It was like our relationship was still the same way it was, if not better, than before I had sucked his dick. I wanted it again though. I just had to have some dick in my mouth again. I even went as far as to make a list of all the guys in the hood that I had to have. I was hooked on sucking dick. I was going to give these niggas the best head they ever had, just as soon as I figured out how to approach them.

I had watched Mike's DVD over and over trying to perfect my oral skills. I had practiced on anything and everything that I could find that resembled a dick. I went through so many of my momma bananas that she thought I was turning into a fucking gorilla. I went on the Internet and found some good step-by-step instructions for dick sucking. I was shocked to find out that it was so much that I didn't know. I learned about trying to keep my teeth out of the way, and the art of deep throating. I knew I was going to be ready next time Mike wanted to get some head from me.

I had just walked out of my house around noon when I heard Shay call my name. Shay was AJ's baby momma and she had just pulled up in her car. She asked me if I knew where AJ was cause she had been calling his phone, but he didn't answer. He was supposed to give her some money for pampers and she needed it right now because she was running late for work. I told her I would go see if he was in his room. I really didn't want to go get him for Shay because I didn't want to hear any of his usual bullshit ass comments, accusing me of being gay. I went ahead and did it anyway because I knew Shay's broke ass really needed the money for pampers.

I walked over to his apartment and the door was unlocked, which was normal. I knew Boo and Mike had left earlier because they called me to see if I wanted to walk over to the recreation center with them. I had to wash my clothes this morning, so I told them I would catch up with them later. I walked inside and AJ's door was closed. I called his name, but I didn't get an answer. I knocked on his door and turned the knob. I opened the door just as AJ was standing on the side of his bed pulling up his pants. He seemed to be in a hurry, and he was sweating really hard.

He just looked at me and said, "What the fuck yo' gay ass want?"

"Nigga yo' baby momma outside and she said she need some money for pampers."

I'm not sure what the fuck happened next, or where the bitch even came from. All I saw was the covers flying off of his bed and a bitch jump up.

"Baby momma? Oh yea nigga? You got a fuckin' baby momma and aint told me shit about that hoe?"

AJ's new girl was clearly pissed the fuck off. AJ and her must have been fucking and that's why he wouldn't answer the phone for Shay. Well I knew he was going to hate me even more than he already did for fucking up his pussy for the day. AJ's girl was still going off on him. She jumped out of the bed and got all in his face cursing at him. When I looked at her all I could say was, "What the fuck!" I knew my eyes had to be playing tricks on me. I must have been dreaming or some shit. I just could not believe what the fuck was happening right before me. All I saw was a big ass dick with a condom on it hanging between *her* legs! AJ's new girl had a fucking dick! She was one of those "nigga-bitches" that AJ had made fun of when we saw one walking to the bus stop one day. He made up his own name for the tranny and called her a *nigga-bitch*, but I just caught AJ fucking a nigga-bitch in his room! Wait, why did the nigga-bitch have a condom on though? She had to be the one fucking AJ in his ass! I was in shock. All I could do was stare at the nigga-bitch with my mouth open. I had never seen one naked before.

I don't really remember what they were saying to each other, all I could hear was a bunch of cursing and screaming coming from the both of them. The nigga-bitch started punching AJ in the head and AJ fell to the floor. The nigga-bitch started stomping AJ with her bare feet! She may have looked like a woman, but she sure did fight like a man! All I remember seeing was two big ol' titties and a dick flopping up and down as the nigga-bitch stomped the dog shit out of AJ. I had seen enough. I had to get out of there. I turned and ran out the front door.

I didn't see Shay or her car when I ran back outside. I guess I was taking too long for her and she had left to get to work. I ran out of the apartments and headed towards the recreation center to meet up with Mike and Boo. On the way there, I couldn't help but think about everything that had just happened. It never crossed my mind why AJ treated me the way he did, even though he had no proof what so ever that I was actually gay. It all made perfect sense now. Clearly it was because of his own insecurities. I would have never in a million years thought that AJ would engage in homosexual activities. AJ was always talking about how much he hated gay people, and here he was getting fucked in the ass by a fucking tranny. I guess he was just trying to keep the spotlight off of him. If AJ hated gay people as much as he claimed he did, why would he care so fucking much that he had to voice his opinion every time he saw one? He wanted everyone to think that he hated gay people so much that no one would ever suspect he was secretly sleeping with men. I thought about that nigga-bitch beating the shit out of him-*I hope AJ doesn't get hurt too badly*!

~   ~   ~   ~

It was around seven that evening when we made it back to the apartments. Mike and Boo went to their apartment and I went to mine. I never mentioned to them what took place earlier that day inside their apartment. If AJ wanted them to know, I thought he should be the one to tell them. I didn't even want to think about it myself. All I could think about was Mike and how I had to have his dick in my mouth again. It had been over a week and I had practiced and researched my techniques. I was anticipating him wanting to get his dick sucked by me again, but he never mentioned it. I figured I would have to make the first move on him this time. I wanted to make sure I was really ready for him, so I went to my room and watched his dick sucking DVD over and over until about midnight. I left out my door on a mission to give Mike some of my good ass head that I knew he would greatly appreciate.

When I walked into their apartment I was surprised to see AJ sitting on the couch. He looked at me and my heart instantly started beating rapidly. I could see scratches on his neck and a big lump on his forehead-*damn that nigga-bitch got him good*!

"Wassup LD?" AJ was unusually calm. He actually called me by my name-he NEVER did that.

"Sup AJ? Where Mike at?"

"Mike left about a hour ago, and Boo in his room sleep. Come sit down right quick."

I was scared now. *What the fuck was he up to?*

"Oh naw, I gotta go back to the house."

"Bro sit yo' ass down so I can holla at ya' right quick."

I reluctantly sat in the chair opposite of him.

"Did you tell anybody about what you saw earlier?"

"No, I aint said nothin' to nobody."

"Good, I would appreciate it if you never mention that shit again bro. That hoe tricked me into thinking she was a girl. I didn't know until it was too late. I aint gay and I don't want nobody thinkin' I'm into that gay shit bro. I don't need these niggas around here lookin' at me sideways and shit. I got two younger brothers that look up to me my nigga. I don't want them to look at me differently because of this bullshit. You feel me? Will you keep this shit between me and you bro?"

AJ was practically pleading with me not to tell anyone about his nigga-bitch that supposedly "tricked" him. That bitch aint tricked his ass into doing shit! As mad as that hoe was, they had to have been fucking around for a while. On top of that, the nigga-bitch was the one who had the condom on! Who in the fuck does AJ think he's fooling with his bullshit ass story? Was that the best he could come up with?

I didn't want to start any problems with AJ, so I agreed to never mention the incident again. I was just surprised that he didn't try to whoop my ass for causing him to get jumped on by that nigga-bitch. I guess it was easier for him to try to keep me quiet than to explain to everyone why he beat me up. Doing that would just risk his chances of me exposing the truth about what really happened to his neck and forehead. I left out of their apartment and started walking around searching for Mike. I was like a crack head searching for his next hit. I just had to suck Mike's dick tonight. I just had to!

Chapter 5

I had walked around for about an hour and still didn't see Mike. I had given up and was walking back to my house when I saw his best friend Chris. Chris wasn't really that cute at all to me. He did have a lot of swag though. He was really tall and dark. He played basketball for the high school so he was really athletic. He had dreams of going to the NBA-*of course,* and was always shooting hoops at the rec. All the neighborhood hoes would go to the court to watch him shoot, hoping that he would pay them some kind of attention and possibly even make one of them his girl. He was really focused on basketball and all the girls in the hood loved that about him. He was always cocky and rude to them hoes too. And yet, they threw pussy at him left and right; mostly for bragging rights.

"Ay Chris, wassup? You seen Mike around?"

"Naw bro, I aint seen him since y'all left the rec earlier."

"Oh ok, where you headed?"

"To chill at the trap."

I had forgot all about the trap! I'm sure that's where Mike was. If Mike was there, I knew I wouldn't get any dick from him tonight. He was going to be busy serving the fiends that knocked on the door all throughout the night, wanting their next fix. Hell I was the fiend tonight! I just wanted somebody, anybody to serve me some good dick so I could get my fix. Shit I was horny and Mike was not going to be able to serve me, so I decided to try my luck with Chris.

My heart started beating faster because I didn't know how he was going to react to my next question.

"You tryna get yo' dick sucked tonight?"

I could hardly breathe as I said it. I just knew he was gon' punch me in my fucking mouth for coming to him like that!

"Hell yea I'm tryna get my dick sucked! Where she at?"

I was extremely nervous now. His dumb ass had no idea who I was referring to! I had already put it out there, so I had no choice but to tell him now.

"Well, umm I meant by me."

He just stared at me in silence. I knew this was it. I tensed up all my facial muscles waiting for him to punch the shit out of me, but surprisingly he didn't. He just continued to stare at me. There was a long awkward silence. Then, out of nowhere he grabbed me by the throat and started choking me! I could hardly breathe! I started gasping for air. He leaned closer to my face and said, "You better not tell nobody that you sucked my dick or I'll beat the shit outta you!"

He let go of my neck and I tried to catch my breath. I was in shock. I thought Chris was crazy now that he damn near killed me, but I couldn't believe that he was actually going to let me suck his dick. *Why the fuck did he have to handle me like that though?* He had made it perfectly clear that if anyone found out about this, my ass was grass! Yea, I was excited to get to show off my skills, but I was also a little concerned. I reluctantly told him to follow me back to my place so I could suck him up in my room. Hell I was horny, and after damn near getting choked to death, I was at least going to get what I wanted from his ass.

We got to my room and Chris took off his T-shirt. I never really noticed his body before, but he was actually sexy. He was tall, dark, and muscular. His abs were off the fucking chain! He even had a six-pack! I was already excited to suck his dick just by looking at his body. He didn't seem nervous at all. He was acting as if this shit was normal for him. I didn't know if he did this before or not, but as calm as he was, it sure did seem that way. He looked at me and said, "You ready to suck on daddy dick?" I just smiled and nodded, "Yes daddy."

I sat on the bed as he walked up to me. He positioned himself in front of me and stood between my legs. He pulled down his boxers, and he was ready for me to eat his meat. I took one look at his dick and sighed; *where the fuck did this nigga dick go?* His dick was on hard, but it was small as fuck. *How in the hell could he be so tall and fine, but have a little ass dick?* His dick did not go with his body at all. It looked like someone had ate his dick before me, and bit the bitch completely off! I was very disappointed, to say the least. He just smiled at me and said, "Come on and suck daddy dick." *What the fuck? Daddy dick? Hell this is more like BABY dick!* I didn't want this crazy motherfucker to choke me out again, so I just smiled and started sucking.

I sucked his dick like it was the last dick on Earth. I used everything that I had taught myself the past week and gave him the best head he ever had. I sucked and slurped, as he moaned and groaned. He even grabbed my head and fucked my throat for a little bit. After sucking on him for about two minutes, he shot the biggest batch of nut I had ever seen in my life. I had caught most of it in my mouth, but some of it got on my face. It was like the fucking levees had collapsed and all of the nut in his body had poured out. He was still moaning and shaking as his little ass dick was resting inside my mouth. I pulled his dick out and spit his nut into a cup I had sitting beside my bed. He was still trying to compose himself when I looked up at him.

He was smiling, "Damn you suck dick good! You suck dick better than these hoes around here."

I started smiling real hard when he said that. "You think I'm that good?"

"Hell yea! That's the best head I ever had. You was deep throatin' and slurpin' all on my shit. Im gon' start callin' you Slurpee!"

We both laughed.

Chris named me Slurpee that night and it has stuck with me ever since. I was pretty excited to hear the positive feedback coming out of his mouth after all the hours of practice I had put in over the last week. However, I wanted to hear that shit from Mike. I wanted to show him that I was actually good at sucking dick. I wasn't ready the first time, but I was going to give him everything "Slurpee" had to offer. I just had to redeem myself for looking like a fool the first time.

Chris had been gone for about an hour when I heard someone knocking at my window. I looked through the blinds and it was Boo. I told him to come to the front door so I could let him in. When I got to the door Boo was visibly shaken up. He was crying and I had never seen him act like that.

"Boo, what's wrong bro?"

He couldn't stop crying long enough to talk. We just stood in the living room, and I tried to comfort him as best I could. I wanted to figure out what the fuck was wrong with him, but I couldn't. He finally calmed down long enough to tell me what was wrong.

He managed to speak between sobs, "Man they just picked up Mike!"

My heart started pounding through my chest. "Who picked up Mike? What are you talking about Boo?"

Tears rolled down his face again as he explained what had just happened.

"The police busted the trap, and they caught him in there!"

It wasn't surprising that the trap had gotten busted; I was honestly shocked that it had taken the police as long as it did to do it. Those words struck me like a ton of bricks. I started crying with Boo. I knew Boo and I were crying about the same situation, but we had totally different reasons for our tears. Boo cried because his brother was being taken away from him for selling drugs. I was crying because I knew I wouldn't get that dick from Mike anytime soon. I was devastated, and crying was the only thing that I could do to ease my pain.

Boo started telling me how he felt as though Mike had been set up. He figured the only person that could have set him up was Chris. Boo told me that AJ thought that it was ironic that Chris was the only person out of the crew that didn't get busted in the trap that night. I felt my heart drop. I couldn't help but to feel nervous after hearing that. I was in a fucked up situation and didn't know how to get out of it. Chris would have gotten busted inside the trap also, if I wouldn't have stopped him on his way and sucked his dick! I couldn't tell Boo that though. All I could do was listen to him. He told me that AJ & his boys went to Chris' house to see what he had to say about the situation. My heart was damn near jumping out of my chest as Boo told me what they were planning to do. I knew if AJ told Dee that he thought Chris had something to do with Mike going to jail, Chris was going to get the shit beat out of him for sure.

Dee hated Chris, only because he took his crown as the best basketball player in our hood. Chris and Dee had a one-on-one basketball match at the rec' one day. I'm not sure exactly what happened, but Chris dunked all over Dee and the crowd went wild. Dee was pissed off that Chris embarrassed him in front of the whole hood, and he has been fucked up about it ever since. Dee was almost twenty and like most of the hood niggas that excel in sports, he fucked up his life after he got his full scholarship to college. All he wanted to do was get high and fuck hoes, so they kicked his dumb ass out. He was once one of the top basketball recruits in the country, but he got to college and just wouldn't do right. Now he's back in the projects trying to convince everyone that he *would have* made it to the pros, but instead he's walking around here getting high everyday and living off his stupid ass baby momma.

Boo wanted us to go around to Chris' apartment to see what was going to happen. I wanted to stay in the house. I couldn't dare be a witness to whatever those boys were going to do to him. I knew I had to be there for Boo though, so I walked around there with him.

We walked up to Chris' apartment just as the ambulance was pulling up. My heart began to race, it was working triple time tonight. I had hoped they didn't do anything drastic to Chris, but I knew better. I knew them well enough to know that they would make him pay even if they only *suspected* him of setting up Mike. All the neighbors were outside and everyone was gossiping. Big titty Betty was on the scene, and if anything went down in our hood, big titty Betty would have the tea for sure.

Big titty Betty was the nosiest bitch in our projects. She knew everybody's business, and didn't mind telling it to anyone who would listen. She was constantly in the middle of some drama and seemed to love her daily arguments with the people around our projects. You couldn't help but hate her and respect her at the same time. She never changed up on you. She was the same messy, big titty bitch day in and day out. I stood closer to her so I could listen in on the conversation she was having with another lady.

Apparently a group of boys came to the upstairs apartment and beat the shit out of whoever opened the door. They heard a bunch of screaming and hollering- something about lying, before the boys finally ran off. I was sick to my stomach. *Why did they have to do him like that?* Chris was fucking innocent and I couldn't even save him from his ass whooping that he shouldn't have even endured. The paramedics were wheeling the body off in a hurry to get to the hospital. Everyone tried to get a look at the body that was on the stretcher. I refused to look at it. I just couldn't see Chris in that condition. I had just given him the best head of his life over an hour ago, and now he's laid out on a fucking stretcher beaten and bruised for nothing.

Just as they were loading the stretcher onto the ambulance, I heard someone say, "There he go!" The entire crowd turned to see Chris running up to the ambulance. *What the fuck was he doing*? I thought he had just gotten his ass beat inside his house, and was being rushed to the hospital! The police were trying to calm him down but he just kept crying and screaming about his momma! That's when I finally realized what the fuck really happened. Them niggas beat the shit out of Chris' momma 'cause they thought she was lying about Chris not being inside the house! Now his momma was the one who got her ass whooped over something that was just a big misunderstanding. I was completely drained at this point. It was always some shit going down in our apartments, but this was too much for me. This dope game bullshit had gone way too far. I started walking home. I heard Boo calling my name, but I was in a state of shock. I just kept walking faster and faster. Eventually I found myself running. I ran all the way until I reached my apartment. I went inside and locked the door. I went to my room and I cried myself to sleep.

Chapter 6

The next morning I woke up to the sounds of kids laughing and playing, and I smelled breakfast in the air. I went into the living room and my little sister and brother ran and hugged me. I hadn't seen them in about three days. I was happy to be around my entire family, considering what had happened the night before. I played around with them while my mom was in the kitchen cooking breakfast. She hardly ever cooked anything, and I was shocked that she was even awake, let alone cooking breakfast this morning. I thought to myself, *She must be in a real good mood*! I was hungry as hell and didn't want to start any arguments with her. I just wanted to enjoy a good meal with my family, which was a rare event within itself.

"Come in here and get yo' plate, the food is ready baby."

Baby? Damn she called me baby! She *must* be in a good mood! Just as I got up from the couch, I saw a man walk out of her room and head toward the kitchen. All this fat ass motherfucker had on was a pair of boxer shorts and some dirty ass socks. *How dare she let some strange nigga walk around in front of her kids like that*! I immediately got pissed off. That didn't stop my ass from getting some of her food though. I was pissed off, but I was still hungry. I went to the kitchen and he was sitting at the table with a plate of pancakes, bacon, eggs, and hash browns. I saw her get two bowls of cereal and set them on the table. *Oh hell naw! I know this bitch was not about to feed these kids cereal after she done fixed this nigga a four course fucking meal*! I went into the kitchen to fix my plate, but I didn't see any more food.

"Where the rest of the food at?"

"Rest of what food? What the hell you talking 'bout boy?"

"The rest of the food you cooked."

"Aint no mo'."

This bitch said that shit, then had the nerve to walk off from me like she didn't give a fuck that I didn't get a home cooked meal.

Then her fat ass nigga had the nerve to jump into our conversation. "Boy you better fix yo ass some cereal or you won't eat shit."

I responded to his fat ass before I even had a chance to think about what I was about to say.

"Bitch who the fuck are you talking to!"

"Bitch? I'll show you who the bitch is little nigga!"

My mom got mad at me and told me to take my ass to my room. I wanted to slap both of they asses in the fucking mouth, and just leave them there with a stupid ass look on they face. This fat ass bitch used our fucking food stamps to cook this nigga a hot meal and wanted us to eat some fucking cereal. I was hot! She had to be out of her fucking mind! I wasn't surprised at all. She will do anything for a fucking nigga, but when it comes to her kids, she always got an issue with it. I couldn't wait 'til I was out of her house and on my own. I made a promise to myself that I would graduate and leave this bitch house and never look back.

Chapter 7

A few years had passed and I had already crossed off five guys I had on my original list of dicks that I must suck. They all loved my head and would come through anytime they wanted just to get it. I felt as though I was a pro now. I was like a dick-sucking machine! I took walk-ins all the time. Sometimes the niggas would pass each other. One would be coming in the door as the other was headed out from getting his nuts drained by my mouth. They didn't give a fuck though. Some of them even knew each other and they would give each other fist pounds as they passed. They already knew what time it was when it came to me. They never spoke about it to each other though. What ever went on in my room stayed between us.

I had continued to suck Chris' dick also. His mother ended up being OK and she actually made a full recovery. They never found out who the niggas were that beat her ass. That wasn't uncommon throughout our projects either. No one wanted to be labeled as a snitch because we lived by the creed that "snitches got stitches!" Anyone that snitched on anything that happened in our hood would risk getting the shit beat out of them if anyone found out who it was that told.

At first I thought Chris wasn't going to let me suck his dick anymore. He came to my house one night and told me that if he hadn't been out with me that night, he probably would have been home to protect his mother. I had to remind him that if he wasn't out with me that night then he would have been at the trap, and he would be in jail with the rest of his crew. I guess he realized how true that was, cause the next thing I knew he was pulling his dick out for me to suck on. I have been sucking his dick ever since then. Hell, he even did some recruiting for me! I sucked him and two of his cousins back to back one night. He had told them all about "Slurpee" and they wanted to try it out for themselves. They were hooked! They would even ride the bus to our apartments just to get sucked up on the weekends!

Boo and I had finally started high school together. All of the coaches wanted us to play for the high school football team. Boo was really excited about playing on the team, but I decided against it. Football just didn't excite me the same way it excited Boo, and I didn't have any desire to play anymore. I wanted to graduate, go off to college, and hopefully become successful through academics. School was my number one priority, and sports took up entirely too much of my free time.

I loved my high school years because it gave me the opportunity to recruit more niggas on a daily basis. Ironically, I started to become more uncomfortable with my sexuality though. I was gay, and I understood that part clearly. I just didn't know how to deal with my sexuality while maintaining my masculinity. I wasn't sure how everyone else would feel about me being openly gay, or how they would even perceive me. I really didn't have anyone that I could actually talk to about being gay either.

There was only one out and proud punk in our high school. His name was Lumpkins, but everyone called him Lump. Lump's mother worked in our school as a security guard. Everyone knew who lump was, and he did get teased sometimes, but for the most part everyone accepted him for who he was. He was feminine acting in middle school, but he turned into a full-blown French-fried faggot when we got to high school. Once everyone figured out he was actually gay and not just feminine acting, they started calling him Lump-the-punk. He absolutely loved that name too! He would wear really tight clothes and twist around the school acting really girly. Now I knew I was gay, but I knew I damn sure wasn't as gay as this queen. He would even get mad if you called him a boy. He wanted to be addressed as *she*. She was always into some drama with the females and just had to be seen wherever she went. She would do things just for attention. I can al-most guarantee that if we went to a funeral, Lump-the-punk would cry the loudest just so she could be seen!

Lump-the-punk couldn't stand me. I really couldn't stand her punk ass either. She was just too much for me. We had mutual female friends and she would be around sometimes when I would talk to them, but we never once acknowledge each other's presence. I think its because deep down, she knew I was gay. No one else knew I was or even suspected me of being gay, so she would make little side remarks every time we would pass each other in the hallways to try to get me to react. One time we passed each other in the hallway and she told her home girl, "Look at *her*." I heard the bitch say that shit and both of them laughed. I wanted to turn around and punch her ass right in the mouth but I ignored him…I mean *her,* or whatever the fuck the bitch wants to be called. She would sometimes yell out, *"Trade"* when I saw her in the hallways also. I would just ignore the bitch and keep moving.

I finally found out what *trade* meant after talking to one of my home girls. She told me that lump had explained to her what trade meant. Trade was a term that gay guys used in reference to guys that appeared to be straight, but would fuck around with other niggas on the down low. Basically, "sheep in wolfs clothing." They would appear to be so hard on the outside, but if you got them in the bedroom alone, they would end up being so soft! I guess all the guys I sucked up over the years would be considered *trade*. Lump thought I was trade too I guess. I never portrayed myself as being straight though. Everyone just assumed I was straight. I knew I was gay and if anyone would have asked me, I would have gladly told them that.

Lump actually stayed in the apartments across the street from mine. Last summer I had seen her walking through our apartments at all hours of the night. I thought she was coming to buy some weed or something. Then the more I watched her, I realized that she had to be on the stroll for some dick. I personally couldn't see who would want to fuck around with her nasty ass. She looked really dirty to me, it seemed as though she didn't bathe or something. I would watch as she would walk by a group of niggas and twist real hard with her ass poked up in the air. No one seemed to pay her any attention, but I'm sure when she caught them by themselves it was a totally different story. I knew these niggas around here and they thought that a nut was a nut. It didn't matter who it came from. All I could hope was that none of the niggas I wanted to suck had ever fucked around with her before. I damn sure wasn't going to suck anybodies dick after her nasty ass!

There were a few guys at school that I wanted to show my skills to. Jay was the quarterback of the football team and I wanted him so bad. He was caramel colored, tall, had tattoos on his chest, and a body that would make a preachers wife look twice! I just had to have him. He sat next to me in science class and I would always help him with his work. He was the typical dumb jock. He wasn't very smart at all and he pretty much depended on my help so he could pass our science class. I didn't mind though, because I knew that if he failed a class he wouldn't be able to play in the football games. In all actuality, I was just trying to get as close to him as possible so that I could make my move on his dumb ass. He did have a girlfriend named Kitty that went to our school. I would speak to her whenever I saw her, but I didn't give a fuck about that hoe. I knew her young ass wasn't sucking his dick like I could, and I was determined to show him what he was missing out on.

I was glad when our science teacher made us pair up to do a group project for his class. Jay made sure I knew that we were going to be partners for the assignment. We had to find time outside of class to work on the project though. Jay did have a car but I really didn't want him coming to my apartments. Them niggas over there were crazy, and if he had any unsettled beef with any one of them, they would surely start some shit if they saw him in our hood. I told him we should just meet up at school one day to work on it. I was willing to do most of the research and let him know what all he needed to do once we met. He was cool with that. I knew he wanted to do as less work as possible and I didn't really trust him to be in charge of a whole lot, so I took control over most of the project. I knew that this was going to be the perfect opportunity for me to make a move on him.

We met up after school inside of the gymnasium. Jay had suggested we go to the gym because he knew it would be empty. I made it to the gym before Jay did, so I just sat in the bleachers and waited for him. When Jay walked into the gym my mouth started watering. He looked so fucking good in his muscle shirt and cargo shorts, with a fresh pair of Jordan's on his feet. Jay had so much swag it was hard not to stare at him.

"Wassup LD?"

"Wassup Jay?"

"Sorry I'm late bro. What all we need to do for this project?"

He was surprised when I told him that I had already completed most of our project and all he would have to do is make signs on a computer and print them out.

"Damn bro! You already got everything done? You the man, fo'real though!"

I just smiled and thanked him. I was glad he was in a good mood cause I wanted to get some of that dick and this was going to be the best time for me to finally let him know.

"What you 'bout to get into Jay?"

"Shit I thought we was gon' be messing around with this project for a minute but you already finished it, so I guess I'm going to the house and chill. What you 'bout to do?"

"I'm 'bout to walk to the house and just chill I guess."

"I can take you home bro, you don't have to walk."

"Where Kitty at though? You not chilling with her today?"

"Man that hoe already at the house, we don't really kick it everyday like that. She aint giving up no pussy so I be out here tryna get it."

Yes! Jay told me exactly what I was waiting to hear. Kitty did seem like she was the type to make a nigga wait for the pussy. I wish they had more girls like her these days. Girls like Kitty made it so much easier for me to talk they niggas into letting me give them head.

"Man you the starting quarterback, you can have any hoe you want."

"Yea, but these hoes all be on that love bullshit. They want a nigga to love them and be with them and shit. I got a bitch already. I just need some good pussy on the side. These hoes don't be tryna hear that shit though. You got a girl LD?"

Damn I didn't think he was gone ask me that shit. I hadn't prepared myself for a question like that. I was supposed to be the one in charge of this conversation, but now he done flipped the script on me.

"Naw I don't have a girl, and I doubt that I will ever have one."

"Man LD it's plenty of hoes out here to go around. Why you think you won't ever have one?"

This was it. I guess this is the right time to tell him. My heart started beating faster and faster. No matter how many times I have told someone this, I always seem to get nervous.

"Well I'm not attracted to females…because I'm gay."

Jay just looked at me. He didn't seem surprised nor did he look disgusted. He just had a blank expression on his face.

"Damn bro, you gay for real?"

I laughed, "Yes I'm for real Jay. I wouldn't lie about being gay."

He laughed too.

"You don't act like a gay dude though. You cool as hell bro."

That was even funnier to me. He said I was cool, which I appreciated, but were gay guys not supposed to be cool? Did being gay make you less cooler than if you were straight?

"Thanks Jay. I know I'm not a flaming fairy or anything, but I'm definitely gay."

Jay just laughed at me. "So are you the one that get fucked, or do you do the fucking?"

Wow! Jay had taken this conversation to another level. I thought I was going to have to bait him in slowly, but he seemed pretty comfortable talking to me about this shit. Truth is I had never actually fucked anyone, and I had never let anyone stick anything up my ass. I had never even thought about doing it either. I was always sucking dick and that's what I liked to do.

"Actually I just suck dick. I love sucking dick, and I have been told by a few niggas that I'm better than these hoes around here."

Jay laughed at me again. "Oh yea? So niggas tell you that you suck dick better than these hoes? Man I don't believe that shit."

"Well you can find out for yourself and you tell me if I'm good or not after I finish."

"Man hell naw LD! You trippin' now bro. I aint gay."

So Jay wanted to play the hard to get game with me. I had a few of them in my apartments that did the same shit, so I already knew how to handle his ass.

"Bro I know you not gay. I aint tryna make you gay either. I just wanna' give you some good ass head. Kitty aint doin' her job so let me take care of that for you. My jaws are way stronger than a females' so you know my head game gon' be off the chain!"

"Man naw LD. I just aint into that gay shit bro."

Damn, He still won't give in! Now it was time for me to pull out the big guns.

"Its not gay if you're the one getting your dick sucked. Jay a mouth is a mouth, so it's just some good ass head. I know you got a girl, and plus I don't suck and tell so don't worry about that. You need to release some stress anyway bro."

Jay sat there quiet for a minute and he just stared at the wall.

"Damn you got me horny now bro! Come on, follow me."

I was excited! I had finally talked his ass into giving up the dick. He really was a dumb jock if he let me talk him into doing this shit that easily. I still had another script I was prepared to use on his ass, but I guess I had said enough.

Jay led me into a small locker room that belonged to the coaching staff. Once we got inside he sat in one of the chairs. I was ready for his meat to be in my mouth. He had me excited about sucking him up and I didn't want to waste another minute. He leaned back in the chair and opened his legs as he looked at me. "Handle yo' business bro."

I dropped right down to my knees as soon as he said that shit. He didn't have to tell me twice. I was ready to eat his meat and see why Kitty dumb ass was neglecting her daily duties. He pulled out his dick for me to suck it. His dick was already on hard and it looked so fucking pretty! It was just a shade darker than his complexion and was about nine inches long. It wasn't too fat and it wasn't too skinny. It was just right. He let out a soft moan as he stuck his dick inside my "pussy mouth". I began to suck his dick as he moaned louder- in ecstasy. He pulled his shorts down all the way to his ankles and said, "Damn this shit feel good! You tryna make me nut huh?" I mumbled, "umm hmm" and just kept sucking on it as I looked up at his face. His facial expressions told me everything that he was thinking. He didn't have to say anything cause the look on his face was priceless. He was enjoying every minute of this and I was too. I sucked and slurped on his dick using a perfect combination of spit, tongue, and suc- tion. I felt as though dick sucking was a science and should not be attempted by anyone that didn't understand the balance of this formula. He was moan- ing loudly and he was almost ready to explode deep inside my mouth.

"Y'all done yet?"

We both jumped and turned to look at the door. The fucking security guard was standing in the doorway. We had been caught! Jay was sitting there with his shorts pulled down to his ankles while I was on my knees between his legs with his dick in my hand! Damn, there was no way in hell we could get out of this shit now. Lump's mother stood there as though she was proud to have busted us doing this gay shit. She had a smirk on her face that said it all. Out of all the fucking guards that patrolled our campus, it had to be this bitch to catch us. She made us get all of our shit together as she called for backup. This had to be the most embarrassing shit I had ever been involved in. I knew right then that this was going to be the talk of the school tomorrow. I just knew this bitch was going to go home and tell her punk ass son and he was gone hold a morning press conference to tell the nation.

They took us to the principal's office and left us there. The principal called Jay in first. Jay had the scariest look in his eyes as he walked into the principals' office. He wouldn't even look at me as he went in. I just sat there and waited. I was so embarrassed. It seemed like everybody on the staff took turns coming into that office just to get a good look at me. The wanted a chance to see the nigga that had just gotten caught sucking dick in the coaches locker room. All I could do was sit there with my head down. Ten minutes later I heard the principal say, "La'Darious step into my office!"

When I walked inside the principal's office I was surprised to see that Jay had already left. I looked around and noticed another door that led out into the hallway and realized that he must have went out that door. The principal had my personal file out on his desk.

"La'Darious this type of behavior is unacceptable in our school. I'm not sure why you would think that it's OK to solicit sex from other male students inside of our school. I have never had any problems out of you young man. I don't know what's going on in your personal life that would cause you to behave in such a manner, nor do I have the time to figure it out. Our football team is respected in this city and I can't have you tarnishing our reputation with these types of inhumane sexual acts! If something is going on at home then I suggest you seek counseling. We have a full time counselor on our staff that will be more than happy to talk to you. In the mean time, I have no choice but to call your parents and let them know that I am suspending you for five days."

I just sat there in a fucking daze. I was trying to soak all of his words in because they hit me like a ton of bricks all at once. Soliciting sex? Tarnishing the football teams reputation? Inhumane sexual acts? I was overwhelmed by all of these accusations. I also didn't like his choice of words that he used to show his dissatisfaction with me. I didn't say a word to him. I knew better than that. I learned to choose my battles wisely. I already knew he wasn't really fond of me after I had chosen not to play football for the school. I definitely wasn't a troublemaker, but he wasn't going to bend the rules for me either. I just sat there and let him do whatever it was that he felt he needed to do. I knew I had to save my energy anyway, because dealing with the wrath of my mother when I got home was going to be a battle within itself.

He used the speakerphone on his desk to call my house. After about six rings my mother finally picked up. She sounded like she already had an attitude, "Hello!"

"Hello, this is Principal Wright, and I am calling to speak to Ms. Bernadine Moss."

"This me."

"Well Ms. Moss, I have your son La'Darious in my office and unfortunately I have to suspend him for five days and I need a parent or guardian to come pick him up from the office."

"Suspended for what? I aint got no damn car to come up to that school!"

"Well Ms. Moss, I would rather speak to you in person about the circumstances surrounding La'Darious' suspension."

"Well I aint got no damn car to come up to that school, and I sure as hell aint walking! So, you need to tell me why his ass done got suspended over this here phone."

"OK Ms. Moss, La'Darious was caught by one of our security guards in a very compromising position with another one of our male students. This type of behavior is unacceptable in our institution and I have no other option but to suspend him for five days."

"Hell I aint heard you say shit that he done did wrong. All I heard you say was a bunch of big ass words that I don't even know the meaning of. What the fuck did he do sir?"

"Ms. Moss I need you to calm down please."

"Calm down? What the fuck do you mean? I am calm. You called my phone waking me up out of my sleep with all this bullshit. Then you gon' set up here and use all these big stupid ass words and shit. Now tell me what the fuck he done went up there and did or I'm hanging up!"

I could see that Mr. Wright was getting fed up with my mother. I already knew her ass was going to act like that. He should have just suspended me and sent me home. He figured out really quickly that he wasn't going to get anywhere with her in the state of mind she was in.

"Well Ms. Moss, your son was caught performing oral sex on another male student."

"What? So you tellin' me, this motherfucka' is a faggot and he up there at that school house sucking dick!"

"Well if that's the way you want to put it Ms. Moss. Like I said before, we have to suspend him for five days and we need a parent or guardian to pick him up."

"Now I done told yo' ass I aint got no dam way up there to pick his dick suckin' ass up! He done stayed up there after school to suck on some fuckin' dicks and missed his dam bus, so he better get here the best fuckin' way he know how!"

*Click

That ignorant bitch hung up the phone in the principal's face. He just looked down at my file and shook his head as he wrote.

Mr. Wright looked up at me and said, "I'm definitely going to recommend that you talk to the counselor upon your return to school next week."

He handed me my suspension slip and I left out of the building. I walked a few blocks away from the school and sat down at the bus stop and cried. I was eventually going to walk the whole way home, but I just didn't have the energy right then. My world was about to turn upside down. Now my mother knew I was sucking dick, and she had to find out in the worst possible way. She even called me a fucking faggot! Tomorrow the whole school was sure to find out, and it would be all around the neighborhood. I was going to be ruined. I was going to be a laughing stock. *Why did this have to happen to me? Why did I have to be attracted to boys? Why couldn't I just be straight like all the "normal" people? This would be so much easier if it was a girl that I had gotten caught with.* I knew I couldn't deal with all the criticism that I was going to endure. I sat there at the bus stop and wanted to throw myself into oncoming traffic and end it all. I figured that would be less painful than what was to come.

After about thirty minutes had passed, I decided it was time for me to make the long walk home and deal with my momma fat ass and all the drama that was headed my way. As I walked home, I heard a car horn coming from behind me. The car pulled up beside me and I looked inside. Jay was behind the wheel.

"Get in LD." I got in the car and he drove off.

"Man LD I didn't know security be coming in the gym like that. I would have never gone in there if I had known. I'm just glad we didn't get in any trouble though."

"What the fuck you mean? Suspension is trouble!"

"Damn, you got suspended bro?"

"Hell yea! You didn't?"

"Naw Mr. Wright just told me to get out of his office and coach will deal with me tomorrow. He told me not to discuss what happened with anyone. He said that he don't want to ever hear about this incident again. That was all he said to me."

"Damn he suspended me and called my momma to tell her I got caught sucking dick. My life is ruined."

I should have known that Mr. Wright would try to cover up for Jay. He was the starting quarterback and he refused to have his athletic department tarnished because of an incident like this. He made it clear that he didn't give a fuck about my well-being or my reputation though.

Jay just shook his head side to side as he drove, "Damn thats fucked up, I didn't know all that bro."

I had Jay drop me off at the rec' center and I walked the rest of the way to my apartment. Jay got my number and said that he still wanted to finish what we started soon, just next time not at the school. Dick was the furthest thing from my mind at that point, but I gave him my number and told him to call me whenever.

I dreaded walking into my front door. I stood outside for about five minutes trying to prepare myself for what was waiting for me on the other side. I don't think I could ever have enough preparation for dealing with the wrath of my mother, so I said fuck it, and opened the door.

When I walked in she was sitting on the couch talking on the phone and smoking a blunt. She looked at me and told whoever she was on the phone with, "Bitch let me call you back. This little faggot motherfucka' just walked through my damn door."

I wasn't at all surprised by her words. I expected all of that coming from her.

She took a puff of her blunt and blew out the smoke. "So you done got yo' ass suspended for suckin' dick at them folks school house huh?"

I just looked at her fat ass. *Why the fuck was she asking me this stupid ass question when the principal already told her what the fuck happened?*

"Punk ass bitch, don't you hear me talking to you?"

I still didn't say anything. I just stared at her. She was really starting to piss me off though.

"When the fuck did you turn into a fuckin' faggot? You've been suckin' dick all this time huh? I should bust yo bitch ass right in yo dick suckin' mouth! You are a fuckin' disgrace to this family! I do all I can for yo' ass and you got the nerve to go up to them folks school house and embarrass me by suckin' dick!"

I had enough of her yelling at me. Before I knew it, I snapped back at her.

"Do you honestly think I *chose* to be gay? Do you think I was given a choice of whether or not I was attracted to niggas?"

"I don't know and I don't give a fuck! What I do know is, you damn sure gon' have to do sumthin bout all that nasty ass shit cause I aint raisin' no fuckin' doo doo chasers under this roof! That must be why yo' daddy didn't want yo' bitch ass! He saw that gay shit in you and ran like a motherfucka'! Hell, if they wouldn't cut my food stamps down I would turn yo' gay ass over to the fuckin' state! Bitch get the fuck outta my face before I beat the shit outta' yo' faggot ass!"

I went to my room and slammed my door. I was shaking so bad. I was hurt, angry and on the verge of a mental breakdown. I just couldn't take anymore of her shit. I sat on my bed and cried. She really hit me below the belt this time. *How the fuck is a dope fiend gone call me a disgrace? That bitch is the only disgrace to this fucking family. My daddy ran out on me? Naw fat ass bitch, he ran out on your dumb ass. He never wanted your fat ass from the start. You were just a fuck to him!* I knew I had to get out of this bitch house as soon as I could. I refused to keep going through all this abuse. There had to be a better life for me somewhere else.

Chapter 8

I fell asleep on my bed and was awaken by a tap on my window. I looked out the window and it was Chris. I told him to come around to the front door. I walked through the house and my mother wasn't there. I wasn't surprised at all. It was time for her nightly hoe stroll. I already knew she would be out all night and sleep all day. That was her daily routine. I opened the door and Chris walked in with his two cousins. I should have known. I already knew where this was headed.

"Say Slurpee, hook us up."

"Naw, not tonight bro, I'm really not in the mood right now."

"Just real quick bro, you know a nigga be feinin' for that good ass head. These niggas rode the bus all the way over here on a school night bro."

"I don't feel like all that tonight."

"Man come on Slurpee, we'll pay you bro!"

Damn they want head so bad that they willing to pay me for it? I knew I was good and all, but damn! I had never thought about making money off my head.

"How much y'all got?"

"We'll give you ten dollars."

"OK, ten a piece. That's gon' be thirty dollars."

They started going through their pockets pulling out money. They started counting their dollars and they came up with twenty-five dollars between the three of them.

"Man Slurpee let us just give you twenty cause they gon' need the other five for bus fare."

"OK, that's cool."

We went to my room and I sucked each of them until they each took turns exploding all over my lips. They all moaned as they took turns fucking my mouth. One would even push my head down on the others' dick as I sucked it. They were true freaks, but they had something I didn't have. They still had their secret locked away safely. I was the only one on the verge of being exposed. It wasn't fair. These niggas were just as gay as I was, but I had to endure all the pain; the stereotyping; the name-calling; the hate.

How could I be mad at them though? It wasn't like it was their fault. They just wanted a nut. I was dealing with my own issues, and it really had nothing to do with them.

They paid me twenty dollars and left. I jumped in the shower and then laid back down in my bed. I wanted to stay inside for the night. I was going to lie there and prepare myself mentally for all of the unwanted publicity I was going to receive once everyone heard about what went down inside the locker room.

~   ~   ~   ~

I tossed and turned all night. I didn't sleep well at all. I had entirely too much going through my mind. I really didn't know how to deal with it all. I looked at the clock and it was 8:15 a.m. I knew all the kids had already boarded the bus and was headed to school.

I knew the rumors were going to spread around the school like a wild fire. All them ghetto ass kids did was gossip all day. It seemed as if they didn't go to school for any other reason. According to statistics, half of the kids wouldn't graduate from our high school anyway. It was just a place for them to go and kick it all day, so the school could receive grant money from the state. The School Board didn't seem to care about the issue as much either. They closed down four high schools in our district to save money. Most of our classrooms had around 40 students with 1 teacher. No one really even cared though. This was the ghetto, and they figured most of the kids here were doomed from the start, so why waste time giving us an education that we won't do anything with anyway.

I put on my clothes and I left the house. I was planning to take the money I made last night and ride the bus all day just to get out and away from my momma. I didn't want to see her fat ass at all. After all the shit she said to me, she could go straight to hell and I wouldn't even give a fuck. I rode the bus to the transit station and jumped on the train to go downtown.

Once I had gotten downtown I took a look around. *Damn there were a lot of people at this station.* Most of them looked as though they were just hanging out though. People were trying to sell all types of shit. They were selling CD's, movies, cologne, and even single cigarettes. There was a lot to see downtown that I had never even known about. It was like a fucking ghetto market place or something. I walked around for a while until I got tired. I walked back to the train station and decided to jump back on the train.

The train to return back home was packed. I got on and sat in the only seat that was left. Just before the train took off, a pregnant lady jumped on just as the doors were closing. She was a cute white lady and she looked about four or five months pregnant. I grabbed her arm as she walked by searching for a seat. I told here she could have my seat cause I knew she needed to rest her feet. She was very thankful and I stood up until a few passengers got off at the next stop. Once we got a few stops down I had realized I was headed in the wrong direction. I didn't mind though. Shit I had no-where to go and I damn sure didn't want to be at home.

I got off at the next station and decided to get something to eat. I went to the burger place that was right next to the train station and I sat inside to eat my food. I looked out the window as I ate. I watched all the people drive by in their fancy cars looking as though they didn't have a care in the world. I could only dream of one day living like that. However, my dream was so far from reality that it was almost ridiculous. As I sat there daydreaming, I heard someone over the restaurants' radio say that being a black man is extremely hard in America. I just wish that I could tell him to try being a gay black man in America and let me know how that works out.

I walked out the door and I noticed a help wanted sign at the grocery store across the street. I decided to go over there and fill out an application. I was turning sixteen next week and I was definitely ready to work. I needed my own money and I needed to save as much of it as I could to get out of that house as soon as possible.

I went to the customer service desk and asked for an application. The lady told me they were hiring for part-time cashiers to work evenings and weekends. That was perfect for me since I went to school in the mornings. She gave me a pen and let me fill it out at the end of the counter. While I was filling out my employment application I noticed a tall light skinned guy picking up his paycheck. He was sexy as hell! All I could think to myself was, *Damn I had to get this job!* I really needed to focus on my application though. That's why my gay ass was in the predicament I was in now-always trying to suck on someone's dick! I really needed to concentrate on my application and quit trying to "solicit sex" as Mr. Wright put it. I just laughed to myself.

I finished filling out my application and I stood in line to hand it back to the lady at the customer service desk. She called me to the front of the line and I handed the pen back to her. She told me to wait and she would call the manager to the front so I could give her my application. I was nervous. I wasn't dressed nor prepared for an interview. I didn't even think they would give me one on the spot. I was thinking they would call me back in a week or so if they were interested.

I waited for the manager to come to the front and when I saw her she looked familiar. She walked towards me and I realized that she was the pregnant lady from the train.

She smiled as she said, "Sir are you following me?"

I laughed, "No ma'am. I wanted to apply for the cashier position that you have available."

She looked through my application.

"Oh great! Have you worked as a cashier before?"

Damn I knew there was a catch. This was just too good to be true.

"No ma'am. I'm fifteen and I'll be sixteen next week so I'm looking for my first job."

"Wonderful! You seem like a nice and polite young man. You were extremely nice to me earlier on the train, and I thank you for that. We need more young men like you in this world. I would be honored to offer you your first job. We actually can hire you at fifteen, so that's not an issue at all. The position pays $8.00 an hour and you would get paid every Wednesday. Would you be available for orientation tomorrow at 5 p.m.?"

I was excited! I couldn't even get the words out to thank her properly. I'm sure that by the way my face lit up she already knew I was overwhelmed with joy. I finally thanked her and damn near hugged her until I realized that would not be professional at all. I was on cloud nine. I walked out of that store and felt like I had moved a mountain in my life. I got back on the train and headed home.

I had time to think about the things that happened to me over the last few days. I began to think that maybe those things were supposed to happen. Maybe everything I had endured yesterday was just an interlude into many more blessings to come my way. The universe was allowing me to go through certain things so that I could come out stronger and wiser. I would not have been at the right place, at the right time, had I not gotten suspended and had the morning off from school. How ironic was it that I was a gay black teen from the hood that had voluntarily done a common courtesy for a white woman, and it actually landed me my first job? I was starting to feel more and more confident about my future as I made the journey back home.

I made it home that evening and I dreaded the walk from the bus stop. I knew by now that everyone at school should have heard about me getting caught, and in true ghetto fashion they had already told their mommas when they came home. I was certain that it should have spread all around the apartment complex by now. As I walked to my apartment I saw a few people that I knew. They all spoke to me as though nothing was wrong. I spoke back to them and I went to my house.

I walked into the house and I was glad to be home alone. I didn't care to see my mother anytime soon. I couldn't take much more of her antics. She was just entirely too much for me to handle. She thought she could go off on her cocaine-induced rants and say whatever the fuck she wanted to say to people and get away with it. She acted as though she owned the fucking world and we were all her employees.

I had been home for about five minutes when I heard a tap on my window. I looked out and seen Boo standing there. I told him to come around so I could let him in. He came inside and he was unusually happy.

"Sup LD? Man I heard about you getting caught at school bro."

"Is that why you're smiling like that?"

"Naw bro I got some good news to tell you."

"Oh ok, does everybody know what happened?"

"Yea pretty much. You know how shit goes around here. Aint nobody trippin' about that shit though. Half the people don't really believe it, and the other half was like shit if that nigga is gay he cool wit me. It's a few niggas that's on that bullshit but you know that's not gon' change. No one knows who the other nigga is though. I don't really care either way. I just wish you had told me that you were gay instead of me finding out like that."

"Yea I know Boo, and I'm sorry you had to find out that way. It's just hard to tell folks shit like that when you don't really understand it yourself. I just never knew how people would react to it. You know that everybody's not OK with being associated with gay people."

"Honestly, I always kind of thought you was gay, but I never questioned it cause I don't give a fuck. You're the same LD to me that you was before I found all this shit out. You know I got yo' back if anybody try to fuck with you too. My nigga you're like family to me. Speaking of family, the good news I had to tell you is that Mike will be coming home next week! I got a letter today from him and he said that he would be getting released next week! Damn I'm crunk! My big bro will be home and we gon' wild out!"

"Hell yeah Boo, we waited damn near four years for this nigga to come home. We have to party like a motherfucka'!"

"Hell yea! I'm bout to go back to the crib though. You should come through if you tryna get yo' ass handed to you in this Madden, no homo."

Boo and I both laughed at his no homo joke as he walked out the door. I was relieved after talking to Boo. He really did care enough about me to still be there for me through all of this. The people at school didn't really seem to care about me being gay either. I guess I was just being insecure. Well hell after my momma pretty much disowned my ass I guess I couldn't blame myself for worrying. I'm glad it turned out not to be as big of a deal as I thought it would be.

I couldn't help but think about Boo's good news. I was excited and nervous that Mike was due to get out of jail next week. He would be home just in time for my sixteenth birthday. I could hardly wait! It had seemed like an eternity since the last time I saw him and had his big, juicy black dick in my mouth. Although, I really shouldn't be too concerned about sucking dick right now, considering everything I just went through in these last couple of days. I just had to have Mike again. I needed to show him how good I have gotten over the years. I was planning to give him the best welcome home head he had ever had!

Chapter 9

I woke up the next morning and I could hear my mother in her room giggling and shit like a little girl. I started to wonder what the fuck was so damn funny until I heard a deeper voice, and I got my answer. This bitch had brought another nigga home. This was the fourth one this week. I was sick of her. All she did all day was get high with these random ass niggas and sleep. This bitch had no drive, goals, dreams, or ambitions. Yet she had the nerve to call me a fucking disgrace. I made it my ultimate goal to never get so comfortable with the way things are, and always strive to make things the way I wanted them to be. Yea we lived in the ghetto, but we didn't have to stay there. I was so glad that I found my new job, and I was going to do everything in my power to make sure I got out of her house as soon as I graduated high school.

I got dressed to leave the house. I didn't have to be at orientation until 5 p.m., but I refused to stay in that house all day listening to her grunting and moaning. I opened the front door to leave, but I had left my ID on my bed. I closed the door and went back to my room to get it. As I walked by my mother's room I heard her say, "Don't worry, that's just my faggot ass son." They both laughed. I just shook my head. Her insults didn't even hurt me anymore. I actually felt sorry for her, rather than for myself. She was so out of touch with reality that it wasn't even funny. Her insults only added fuel to my fire, and I knew I had to try extremely hard to make a way for myself.

I got downtown and I had a little time to waste before I had to be at orientation. I decided to walk the streets again. I walked around looking at all the skyscrapers and imagined myself one day walking into one of them with a suit on, while holding my briefcase. As I was daydreaming I heard someone say, "Excuse me sir." I turned around to see who it was and it was a guy with an all white uniform on.

"Sorry to bother you sir. I am Petty Officer Lewis and I am a recruiter with the U.S. Navy. I would like to chat with you if you have time."

"Umm sure, I have time. What do you want to chat with me about?"

"Well I wanted to talk to you about everything the Navy could offer you. By the way, what is your name sir?"

"Well my name is La'Darious, but everybody calls me LD."

"OK LD, would you mind stepping into my office so we can talk about everything that the Navy has to offer you?"

"Sure, I have a few minutes to spare."

Once I got into his office I was asked to fill out an information sheet with my name, address, telephone number, school name, and parents information. Petty Officer Lewis was extremely nice to me. He grew up in the Dallas area and he told me that joining the Navy saved his life. He didn't know where he would be right now had he not joined the Navy while he was in high school. He told me that I could travel the world and visit foreign countries for free, go to school for free while I was in the Navy, and I would still get money for college if I decided to get out. He told me I would get paid twice a month, and I would also get thirty days of paid vacation a year. Most of all, they would give me money to pay my rent if I got my own place.

I was excited, but I was also a little scared. I didn't want to go to war. I didn't know much about the Navy personally, but I knew they were apart of the military and would definitely go to war if needed. He told me to take some time and just think about it. Also, to expect a call from him in the near future to check on me and see how things were going. I took his card and left out of his office. I needed to hop back on the train and head to orientation.

It was three of us inside the training room waiting for the manager. I couldn't help but notice that I was the only black person there. I was also the only guy. The other two white girls obviously knew each other because they were talking and laughing the whole time. I just sat back and waited for the manager. I wanted to focus all of my attention on what ever they were about to tell us. The manager walked in and introduced himself. Ken was an older, obese white guy with ten years of service to the company. He walked us through our company handbooks, and gave us uniform items to wear during our shifts. After we filled out all the paperwork, he took us on a tour around the store. I was surprised to see how much was going on behind the scenes of a grocery store that I never knew about. The last stop of our tour ended up being in the break room. Ken placed us on a fifteen-minute break and asked us to find our way back to the training room to complete our orientation once our fifteen minutes were up.

I was sitting inside the break room reading a magazine when I noticed the sexy guy that I had seen picking up his check walk in. He looked so fucking good to me! He walked in and sat down at the table. He looked at me and threw his head up in the air as his way of saying *what's up*. I got up and walked toward him to shake his hand.

"Wassup? I'm La'Darious, but everybody calls me LD."

He shook my hand and said, "I'm Antonio, but everyone calls me Tony. I never seen you around here bro, are you new?"

"Yea today is my first day. I'm in orientation right now."

"Oh that's wassup bro. What's your position?"

"I'm a cashier. What's your position?"

"I'm a stocker. I've been here for almost a year. It's a pretty chill place to work. It has its ups and downs, but I like it for the most part. Welcome aboard!"

"Thanks. I better get back up here to orientation before I'm late."

"OK LD, I'll see you around."

I made my way back to the training room. I was the first one back too. The other two girls walked in five minutes after our fifteen-minute break was over. Ken wasn't too happy with them, but he let them slide since it was our first day. We had to watch a few more movies about the company. After that, he handed us our training schedules and released us around 9 p.m. I had to work the next day from 5 p.m. – 10 p.m. I was excited that I was finally getting a chance to do my job and make my own money.

It took me about an hour to get home. I thought about Tony the whole ride there. I wondered if he had a girlfriend and how big his dick was. I wanted to know if he was circumcised and how big his nuts were. I wanted him bad and I was going to do everything in my power to suck his dick.

I walked from the bus stop and noticed the ambulance pulling into my apartments. I wasn't surprised at all. There was always some shit going down over here. The police and ambulance were over here almost every day. I walked to my apartment and noticed that they were parked in front of my unit. In true project fashion, there was a big crowd of people standing outside being nosey. I started looking for big titty Betty so I could get the scoop on what happened. Before I could even get up to the crowd, Boo came running up to me. He had tears in his eyes.

"Bro I been looking all over for you!"

"Why? What's wrong Boo?"

Boo just looked at me and shook his head as tears rolled down his face. "Bro it's yo momma!"

"Huh? What the fuck happened to her?"

I couldn't wait for Boo to respond. I ran up to the ambulance as they were loading her into the back. A police officer grabbed me as the paramedics closed the door to the ambulance and drove off.

I tried to fight my way out of the officer's grip. I started yelling at the officer, "That's my fucking momma in there!"

"I understand sir, but I need you to calm down for a minute. I need to let you know what's going on, but I can't if you're going to continue to be aggressive."

"Sir just tell me what the fuck happened to my momma!"

"Well your mother passed out due to a drug overdose. The paramedics were able to revive her and they believe she is going to be fine. They are taking her to the county hospital for further observation and treatment."

All I could do was get angrier and angrier as I replayed his words in my mind. I just looked at the officer and said, "A fucking drug overdose?" This bitch had the whole projects out here watching us, my best friend crying his fucking eyes out, and was about to make me have a heart attack all because she did too many fucking drugs! I just walked away from him shaking my head and went inside the house.

I locked the door and I looked around the living room. I looked on the coffee table and saw cocaine residue, two cigars, and a bag of weed. I just shook my head. This bitch had outdone herself this time. I couldn't help but laugh and worry at the same time. This bitch runs me in the ground about being gay every chance she gets and now she is laid up in the hospital without any support. She was still my mother regardless, but I refused to go see her in the hospital under these circumstances. She clearly needed help, and hopefully the doctors and nurses at the hospital would convince her of that.

I cleaned up the living room and flushed all the drugs I had found down the toilet. I went outside to see what everyone was doing. I went to Boo's house and no one was there. I looked at my watch and I figured that he went back to the rec' considering there was still thirty minutes left before it closed. As I walked to the rec', I saw Chris leaving from there and he was walking towards me.

"Wassup Chris? Did you see Boo at the rec'?"

Chris just kept walking towards me. *Clearly he didn't hear me.*

"Chris! Did you hear me?"

He got a little closer and said, "Gay ass nigga don't say shit to me!"

I was confused. *I know this nigga didn't just call me gay and tell me not to say shit to him!*

"Who the fuck are you calling gay?"

"Yo' bitch ass! Nigga you gettin' caught suckin' niggas dicks and shit at the school. You out there bad bro! Don't say shit else to me! You better get the fuck out of my face before I beat yo' gay ass too!"

I was pissed now! Not only did this nigga call me gay and tell me not to ever talk to his ass again, but he had the nerve to say he was going to beat the shit out of me! I saw AJ, Boo, and Dee walking towards us, so I knew it was about to go down.

"Oh yea nigga? You gon' beat my ass like them niggas beat the shit out of yo' bitch ass momma huh?"

The look on his face was priceless. If looks could kill, I would surely be dead! Chris dropped his basketball on the ground and swung at my face. I ducked and he grabbed me and threw me to the ground. AJ, Boo, and Dee were on top of his ass before he even had a chance to punch me. We all beat the shit out of him! We stomped, kicked and punched on him until he passed out. Then we all took off running to the apartments before anyone saw us. We ran to my house and we all went inside.

We were out of breath, but we were laughing and talking about how we just beat the shit out of him. AJ asked me why we were fighting in the first place. I had to think of a lie quick. I told him that I had asked Chris if he knew Mike was getting out of jail next week. Chris said something about "fuck Mike", and the argument between us started from there. They were clearly satisfied with that lie that I had made up off the top of my head. They felt even more satisfaction about beating his ass now that they thought it was in Mike's honor. We laughed about it until they all left.

I was awakened out of my sleep that night because the phone was ringing. I looked at the caller ID and saw that it was the hospital, so I answered.

"Hello?"

The voice sounded really drowsy and low, but I could tell it was my momma.

"LD, what are you doing?"

She spoke slowly and it seemed as though it took forever for her to get out those words.

"I was sleep until the phone woke me up."

"Well make sure you put my drugs up that's in the living room. Nobody betta' not smoke my shit up!"

I didn't know if this bitch was delirious from the medication or what. She was lying up in the hospital due to a fucking drug overdose and could barely talk. Yet, she wants to call me in the middle of the night demanding that I take care of her damn drugs until she gets home! I was disgusted!

"You need to get some help! You fucking dope fiend!"

"Listen here you little gay ass…

–click

I just hung the phone up in her face. There was no way in hell she was going to belittle me over the phone, in the middle of the night, and expect me to just sit there and listen. I rolled over and went back to sleep.

The next day I woke up in a really good mood. I didn't have to see my mother's face and I had a job to go to. I was feeling good. I cleaned up my room and ironed my work uniform. I heard the phone ring and I looked at the caller ID and saw the hospital number again. I answered the call, "Hello?"

"LD?"

It was my mother again.

I yelled, "Get some help!"

I hung up. I was not going to let her ruin my day with her bullshit. I was not about to enable her addiction either. If she wanted those drugs that bad then she would have to chase them through the sewer lines.

I got dressed for work and went to catch my bus. I arrived at the train station and the train was already there. It felt like it was there waiting just for me. Yea I knew it was scheduled to be there at specific times, but today I felt as though it was personally waiting for me to board before taking off.

I was excited about my first day on the job. I was going to be making my own money and begin setting myself up for success. I must have been smiling to myself just thinking about my job because an old lady was staring and smiling back at me once I stopped daydreaming. I laughed to myself and enjoyed the rest of the train ride to my new job.

Once I got to work I was placed with a trainer to teach me the ropes and help me understand how the cash register worked. They had a cash register inside of a classroom where she taught me all the things I would need to know before I actually went out on the floor. I could practice all I wanted until I felt as though I was ready to check out real customers. She took me around the store to show me where everything was located just in case a customer ever asked me for something. The last stop was the produce section where she encouraged me to spend some time learning all the names of the fruits and vegetables. She told me that I would have to know their specific codes assigned to them in order to check out customers. She handed me a sheet of paper and told me to familiarize myself with the common fruits and vegetables that were on the list. She gave me twenty minutes to look around and told me to meet her back in the training room once I was done.

While I was looking around, Tony came out of the storeroom to restock the fruits and vegetables. I went over to him to keep him company.

"Wassup Tony?"

He looked at me and smiled-*Damn he had some pretty teeth*!

"Wassup LD? How you likin' training so far?"

"So far so good. I can't complain at all."

We continued talking until a skinny black chick interrupted us. She had baby blue hair, and long, curved, lime green nails. She looked at Tony and said, "Damn you fine!"

Tony just smiled and said, "Thank you ma'am."

"You're welcome baby. I'm looking for the micro-wavable *sarshits and bistits*."

Tony and I looked confused. Before we had a chance to respond she said, "Y'all know what I'm talkin' bout, the microwavable breakfast sandwiches."

Tony replied, "Oh! Ma'am the *sausage and biscuits* are on aisle 3."

She said, "Thank you baby" as she walked off.

Tony and I looked at each other and burst out laughing. We were laughing so hard that we had to go to the back before we caused a scene in front of the customers. We laughed for almost five minutes at her. Tony seemed to be a pretty cool person. I wanted to know more about him though. He was sexy just like the lady had said, and I'm sure he had a girl, but I didn't care though. I had to have him and I was going to make sure we became the best of friends so that I could eventually get all the dick I ever wanted from him.

I went back to my trainer and finished up for the night. She was satisfied with everything I had learned. She told me that I seemed to be a natural fit for working the cash register. I practiced greeting customers and she said that I caught on to the basics quicker than anyone she had ever taught. I was happy to hear that. I was glad I found something that I could excel at and make money doing at the same time. I took my cash register handbook home with me because I was going to study for the rest of the night and be ready for everything she was going to go over during my next training session at noon.

I made it home around 11 p.m. and I just wanted to shower and study. I looked through the caller ID to see what calls I had missed. I saw a few numbers that I didn't recognize and also a call from the U.S. Government. *The U.S. Government?* Now I know they don't just call your house to say hi! I didn't know who that could have been or what they even wanted, but it made me nervous just thinking about it. The hospital number showed up seven times. I knew that my momma had issues but she was clearly out of her mind. I really hoped they would make her go to rehab so she could clean herself up. I couldn't take much more of her shenanigans.

As I was going through my caller ID, the phone rang again. I didn't recognize the number at all, but I answered it anyway.

"Hello?"

"LD there?"

It was a female's voice on the other end.

"This me."

She jokingly said, "Hey bitch what you doin'?"

I laughed and said, "Who is this?"

"Bitch this Red!"

I knew exactly who she was now. Red was one of my home girls from school. Red was a sexy light skinned chic and she had fucked half of our school-*male and female*. She was the biggest hoe, and she knew it. She didn't seem to care either way. She was ready to fight at the drop of a dime and would beat down any hoe or nigga that would step to her. Please don't let her hear that somebody had been talking about her behind her back. She would march right up to them and confront them in front of everybody. She had gotten kicked out of middle school for ramming a teacher's head into the chalkboard. She didn't play and everyone knew she was crazy. Some would even call her bipolar. She was cool with me though. I laughed and talked to her all the time. I just never gave her my phone number so I was wondering what the hell she wanted.

"Oh hey Red, how you get my number?"

"Boo gave it to me today."

"Oh ok, well wassup with it?"

"So bitch you been holdin' out on me?"

"What you mean?"

"I heard you got caught suckin' dick. You aint never told me shit about you bein' gay."

We both laughed.

"Umm well you never asked me."

"Bitch you shoulda' been told me that. You know I love to hear nasty ass sex stories. Who did you get caught with? I hope he had a big dick!"

"Red now you know I can't suck and tell. It goes against everything I stand for-well kneel for in this case. I wanted his dick bad though, so I guess that meat was worth getting caught over."

We both laughed again.

"Well bitch I want you to go somewhere with me tomorrow night. Don't get all scared and shit, but it's a gay club called Vaseline Alley and it be crunk on Saturday nights. I know the lady at the door so she'll let us in for free and she won't even check for ID's. It's boys and girls in there so we can both have fun. You goin' bitch?"

I was trying to digest everything she had just said to me. There was a *gay* club here in Dallas and she wanted me to go with her? I had never been to a gay club before and didn't even know we had them here. She was taking me way too fast. I needed her to slow it up just a little. I had just been ousted to the world and I'm already getting gay invitations. I wasn't even comfortable being gay yet, so I knew I wouldn't feel comfortable being inside a gay club. I didn't know what to say.

"I don't know about all that Red."

"Bitch come on. You gon' make me fight you!"

We both laughed and I said, "How are we supposed to get there?"

"I'm goin' to get my friend to drive us. She has a car so we'll be good. Come on LD you'll have fun! I just want us to go out and dance and have fun together."

I thought about it for a minute. *What would I have to lose at this point? Everybody knows I'm gay now so it aint like it's going to be a big deal.* I sighed and said, "Ok Red, I'll go. What time do I need to be ready?"

"Yay! We gon' have so much fun bitch! We should be there to pick you up around 10:30 tomorrow night."

I said, "Ok, I'll talk to you later" and hung up the phone.

I was kind of nervous about going to a gay club for the first time. I didn't know how I was supposed to act, what I was supposed to do, or what to even wear. I thought about what it would be like to be under a roof with a bunch of punks and dikes. The more I thought about it, the more nervous I got. I jumped in the shower to try to relax and ease my mind before I studied my handbook for training the next day. I needed to clear my mind so I could memorize all the produce codes and be able to work the real cash register as soon as possible.

Chapter 10

I woke up early so that I could go over my handbook before my training class started at noon. I wanted to learn everything I needed to know in order to move the training portion along as quickly as I possibly could. I needed to be out on the floor so I could mingle with the customers everyday. It was around 9:15 a.m. when I heard the phone ring and I saw the hospital's number on the caller ID. *What does this dope fiend want now?* I reluctantly picked up the phone.

"Hello?"

"Hello this is Dr. Shaw and I was trying to reach La'Darious Moss."

"This is he."

"Hi La'Darious, sorry to bother you so early but I had been trying to reach you all day yesterday without any luck. I just wanted to call and give you an update on your mother's condition. Is this a good time for you?"

"Yes sir it is."

"Well she is doing great here with our staff and I expect her to make a full recovery. I do think that her drug addiction needs to be addressed and this is something that should be rectified immediately. We are going to place her in our onsite treatment facility so that she can get the help that she so desperately needs. She has agreed to go through treatment with our specialists and will be placed into the facility Monday morning. Her participation in the program is voluntary and she has the right to leave anytime she wants. That's why I wanted to encourage you and your family to give her all the support and love she needs to make it through and complete this sixty day program."

"Oh ok sir, thanks for the update."

"You're welcome La'Darious. So can I count on you and your family to support your mother throughout her treatment?"

"We'll see what we can do doctor."

"Great! Hope to see you all visiting her soon."

"Ok doctor, you have a good day."

"Thank you La'Darious. You enjoy your day as well."

I hung up the phone and was glad that conversation was over. It started to get a little awkward for me. He wanted her family and friends to support her during her treatment, but she didn't have anyone that actually cared about her or the fact that she was seeking help. She didn't have many friends and the ones she did have were dope fiends too. They damn sure weren't going to support her effort to get clean. The only family we had left hated her guts. She had found some kind of way to fuck over our family members in any and every way imaginable, so she wasn't going to get any support from them. I was really the only person she had left, and I wasn't really in her corner right now either. The way she treated me when I needed her love and support was more than enough for me to give up on her.

It's sad to say, but at this point I really didn't care if she finished the treatment or not. Even if she did finish, she was going to come back to these same projects and run around with the same people, so eventually she would be back doing the same things. She had been on drugs for so long that it didn't even seem normal for her to be sober. I wasn't going to waste my time trying to support her when I know she would be getting high less than a week after she got home. The doctor was just going to have to find another cheerleading section for her, cause I wasn't going to be there.

I made it to work around 11:30 that morning so I had a little time to spare. I went into the break room and saw that Tony was there going through his cell phone.

"Wassup Tony?"

"Wassup LD? You know how to work this cell phone?"

"Unh unh, I don't even have a cell phone."

"I just got mine today from the lady in front of the store. They give you a free cell phone and the service is only $40 a month. You don't even have to pay anything right now cause they will just take $10 out of your paycheck every week."

"Damn that's a good ass deal!"

"Yea I know! She still out there, go get you one bro."

"Ok."

I went to the front of the store to sign up for the cell phone service and was glad I did. I always wanted a cell phone. I would see the stars on TV with their phones up to their ears, walking around with their shades on and I wanted to do that too. It only took five minutes for me to sign up for my phone and get it activated. I went back into the break room and showed Tony what phone I had gotten.

"We got the same phone LD. That's what's up! When you learn how to work yours, you can teach me."

I laughed as I looked through the owners manual, "Ok, just as soon as I figure this shit out I'll help ya."

"What's yo number so I can save it in my phone?"

I got excited! *He asked me for my number!* This phone was already bringing me good luck and I hadn't even had it ten minutes yet! We exchanged numbers and programmed them in our phones. It was ironic that both of us worked noon to six today and we were both off on Sunday. I was glad to get a chance to see him today and now that I had his number I could "solicit sex" from him off of the companies time. We both clocked in at noon and started our shifts.

I blew right through the training class. I had memorized everything in that handbook and the trainer was very impressed. I even memorized the list of common produce codes she had given me. She kept saying that she thought I was ready to go out on the floor because I had already learned everything that she had to teach me. She talked to the front-end manager and they let me go out and sack groceries for an hour to observe the flow of the cashiers. I went back into the training classroom to take my test before it was time for me to go home. I passed the test and only got one question wrong. It was a question about buying hot food on food stamps. I had skipped that section of the handbook, because I thought I was a expert on that particular subject. I assumed that it was possible because the corner store by our apartments let us do it all the time. I didn't know that was illegal until the trainer explained it to me. Other than that, I was ready to start on the floor and I was going to get my chance Monday evening. The trainer told me to enjoy my weekend and be ready Monday at 5 p.m. to officially start cashiering.

I left work happy that evening. I had a great job and worked with great people and I was really starting to be happy with myself. During my bus ride home, I went through my phone trying to figure out all the features it had on it. As I was doing so I received a call from Tony.

"Hello?"

"Wassup LD? You figured out how to work this phone yet?"

Damn he sounded good over the phone. He had a deep, sexy voice and even if you never met him, you knew he just had to look good once you heard him talk.

"Naw not yet, I was goin' through it when you called. I'm on my way home now."

"Oh you must stay far! I've been home for about thirty minutes now."

"Well I have to ride the train back to my side of town and then catch a bus that takes me to my apartments."

"Oh ok, I live right down the street from the job. What you doin' tonight?"

I had to think about that question. I had damn near forgot about the gay club with Red. I had been so busy durin' training that I almost forgot about my début at the gay club tonight.

"I'm goin' out with my friend tonight. What you got planned?"

"Nothing much bro, just trying to see what I can get into tonight. Well I'll hit u back in a few LD, my girl calling on the house phone."

"Ok bro."

I knew he had to have a girl, and now he had just confirmed it. He looked so fucking good and I knew these hoes would throw themselves at him every chance that they got. I expected him to have one, but that wouldn't stop me from pursuing my goal with him.

When I made it home there was a note on my door that said U.S. Navy on it. I read it and realized that it was from Petty Officer Lewis, the recruiter that had stopped me downtown. He said he had called me a few times and wanted me to give him a call to discuss my future plans. I sat the note on my dresser and went through the caller ID. I saw that U.S. Government number again and figured out that it was Petty Officer Lewis who had been calling me from that number.

I called Red from my cell phone and told her she can start calling me on it from now on. She said we were still going out and she was ready to party. I was ready to party also, but I was still nervous and confused about the whole thing. I was definitely going to go though.

Tony called me back that day, as he had promised. We talked for about two hours over the phone. He turned out to be very smart and we actually had a lot in common. He told me that his current family adopted him at a very young age and that he has never known who his real parents are. He said that he did have a girlfriend and they had only been together for a month. She was already accusing him of cheating on her and he didn't think they would last long at all. I told him I was sorry to hear that, but I was secretly glad she was insecure. That would make my job so much easier.

I told him my story about my deadbeat dad and my dope fiend mother. I got carried away during our conversation and ended up telling him how my mother treated me when she found out I was gay. He didn't even act weird about it either. He was really apologetic about all of it. He assured me that he didn't have any issues with gay people at all. He told me to pray for my mother and hopefully she would accept me for who

I was in the future. He even tried to encourage me to go see her in the hospital. I refused his advice though. He told me to just take some time to think it over, and that hopefully I would be able to find some forgiveness for her so that I could eventually visit her in her time of need. We talked until our cell phone batteries ran down. We both had to put our phones on the charger so we ended our phone call.

The time really flew by when I was talking to him and I enjoyed every minute of it. That was the first time that I had actually had an extended phone conversation with a guy that I had actually been attracted to. He was smart, funny, caring and down to earth. The only problem was that he was straight-at least for now he was. I knew better than to think that he would want anything more than a friendship from me, but I would take whatever it was that he was willing to give.

Red picked me up at 10:45 and I was surprised to see that she had Lump in the car with her. My first thought was to turn around and go back inside, but I didn't want to be rude so I got in the car and went with them anyways. Lump spoke to me when I got in the backseat with her, so I spoke back. We really didn't say much to each other the whole ride there. I was glad that Red's home girl had the music blasting; we couldn't talk over all that bass coming from her trunk if we wanted to.

When we got to the door at Vaseline Alley I had a few butterflies in my stomach. I was anxious but nervous to see what was going on inside a gay club. Once we got inside I started looking around. I was aware that gay people existed, I just had never seen so many under one roof before! It was like I had entered into a secret society and everyone was comfortable with who they were.

Most of the guys reminded me of Lump. They were really punkish with small shirts and tight jeans on. The majority of the girls looked like thuggish ass dudes though. Most of them were all hugged up with pretty model-looking girls. The boys were hugged up with each other too. They were kissing and grinding all on each other. I had never seen anything like it in my life. I felt like an outcast because I was shocked that people were carrying on like this in public. Yea I was sucking dick every chance I got, but it was done privately. I never would have thought it was ok to show my affection for another man publicly. I didn't even know how to react to it. I didn't want to stare but I had to get a good look at everything.

The night went by pretty quickly. They had performers that would come out on stage and lip sync to the songs of their choice. People would actually walk up to them and give them money for doing it too. I saw a few nigga-bitches there and they performed also. They seemed like they were all having a blast. Lump was all over the club when they opened the dance floor up after the shows were over. He was dancing and sweating really hard. He seemed to be having the time of his life. There were a few fights also. From what I was told, the fights were because of females fighting over other females that they were no longer with, but hated to see them with a new girl. We still partied though despite all of that.

We left the club when it closed at two that morning. I actually had fun. If I went again I would definitely not be as scared as I was this time, and may even dance a little more. Lump was still crunk as we walked back to the car. He had gotten some guy number and he was really excited about it. Lump told us that nigga had no choice but to give up the digits after he saw how good Lump could shake her ass. We all laughed. Lump seemed cooler than I thought. I guess I just couldn't see that because I wasn't looking past his gay exterior. He had us laughing the whole ride home.

I woke up the next day and made myself some breakfast. I didn't have to be at work so I was just going to relax and chill. I went outside to see if anything was going on. No one was out so I went back inside to play with my cell phone.

I watched TV for a while then I heard a knock at the door. I opened the door and it was Lump. I let him in.

"Wassup Lump?"

"Hey bitch! So did you have fun last night or what chile?"

"Yea, I actually enjoyed myself."

"The niggas were all on me! Did you see them choosin' me LD?"

I laughed, "Yea I saw 'em all over you!"

"So what's yo' tea LD?"

"What you mean by that?"

"Bitch what's yo' story. Why are you gay? You a top, bottom, or verse? C'mon bitch, give me the skinny!"

I looked at him and laughed as he sat down on my couch waiting for me to answer all his questions.

"C'mon LD, I came over here for the tea so po' me up bitch! I want my cup to runneth over honey!"

I laughed at Lump again. He was a true comedian and he seemed to make everything into a joke.

"Well I have always been gay for as long as I can remember. I always have been attracted to guys. I sucked my first dick when I was twelve and I have been hooked ever since."

"Damn bitch! Twelve? You was a young filthy queen huh?"

We both laughed.

He asked, "So are you a top, bottom, or verse?"

"Umm I don't even know what that is."

Lump explained to me what they each meant. A bottom was the guy that liked to get fucked. A top was the guy that liked to do the fucking. A verse was someone that would do either one depending on the preference of the other guy they were having sex with. I had never had anal sex so I wasn't sure what category I would fit into.

"I have never had anal sex before."

"Girl! So no one has taken a trip down yo' Hershey highway honey? So you tellin' me that all you do is suck dick?"

"Yea, I have never done anything else or even wanted to."

"Bitch you don't know what you missing! I'm a bottom and I love when these niggas climb on top of me and beat my back in. Makes me feel like real fish!"

I didn't know how to feel about all that. I was happy and content with sucking dick. Lump was introducing me to a whole other side of being gay that I had never experienced.

"Doesn't that hurt your ass hole?"

"Well the first time it does. If you tell him to go slow and lube his dick up really good it will eventually open up and he can fuck you like he fucks fish."

"Who is fish?"

"Damn bitch are you really gay or is this a fuckin' activity for you? You must be one of those part-time fags honey. You don't know shit huh?"

We both laughed. Lump explained some of the gay lingo to me. He told me fish was the name we used for real females. He gave me tips on how to position myself the first time I ever let someone fuck me so it wouldn't hurt as much. He even told me how to clean my hole out so that I wouldn't paint trade. He told me that painting was gay lingo for leaving residue on a guy's penis after they have fucked you in the ass. He said the worst thing to be known as in the gay community is a painter. He also explained that we were able to use words like punk, queen, and fag amongst each other because we didn't mean any harm behind it. However, the minute any piece of trade called himself calling us a fag we were obligated to attack! We laughed and talked some more. I realized that Lump was actually cool and he was much more likeable than I first thought. He had me speaking gay lingo after a while. I realized that he had asked all these questions about me, but I didn't know anything about him.

"So what's yo' tea Lump?"

"I don't really like to discuss my tea with strangers honey!"

We both laughed.

"I told you mine, now it's your turn."

Lump looked as though he really didn't want to tell me, but he went ahead and told me anyways. He told me that his stepfather began molesting him when he turned four. His mother knew what was happening to him, but did nothing to stop it. It went on for years, and he finally told his teacher at middle school, thinking that would help the situation. The teacher didn't help him at all. Instead, the teacher started molesting him inside the school's bathroom!

"Damn, I'm sorry to hear that."

"It's cool LD. I used to wonder what did I do that would make these men want to fuck me all the time like they did. I would even question God and ask him why he would allow this to happen to me. It took me some time to realize that it wasn't my fault at all. They were just sick men that wanted to have sex with little boys by any means necessary."

"Did they ever get caught?"

"Yeah they did. I had tried to kill myself in the seventh grade and that's when everything came out in the open."

"Damn it was that bad that you wanted to commit suicide?"

"Yea, at the time it was. I was young and dumb. I didn't have anywhere else to turn to. My mother allowed the shit to happen to me. I thought my teacher would help me, but he ended up doing the same shit that I was trying to stop! I felt at the time that death was my only way out."

"Damn Lump, that's really sad. That's good they got caught, but that doesn't make you whole again. You still have to live with all that abuse though. The way you and your mother act at school, I would have never thought that she allowed you to get molested by your stepdad."

"She's not my mother. CPS took me away from my mother and my aunt adopted me. That's when I moved over here with her. She has raised me since the seventh grade. I don't know where I would be if it wasn't for her."

"Oh ok, I'm really glad everything worked out for you. Let me ask you a question though, if you went through all that sexual abuse with men for as long as you did, why are you attracted to them now?"

"I guess because that's all I know. I have been pleasing men sexually for so long that it seems natural to me at this point. I tried to have a girlfriend in middle school. I even kissed her once. That shit felt so weird though. Fuck all that shit Katy Perry talking bout in her song. I kissed a girl and I damn sure didn't like it!"

Lump had a way of turning every damn thing into comedy. I was enjoying our conversation so far.

"How did you become comfortable being openly gay?"

"Well initially it was my way of acting out. I was doin' this as a way of asking for help. I was in the seventh grade when I started acting this way and I was hoping someone would step in and try to see if anything was wrong with me. They never did though. It had gotten to the point to where I couldn't take it anymore and I swallowed a whole bottle of Tylenol tryin' to kill myself and I passed out at school."

"Wow Lump that's really sad to hear."

"Yea the worst part about all of it is that my own fuckin' mother allowed him to do this shit to me, and she wouldn't even do anything about it. She wanted a fuckin' man by her side so bad that she let him rape me and she just acted as though nothin' was happening. It had gotten so bad that she even started hating me because he wouldn't fuck her anymore. He would always come home high and fuck me on the weekends and she would just act like she was in her room sleep."

"Im glad you're much better off now that your aunt has adopted you. That's so fucked up Lump. I don't know what our mothers are thinking by staying with these low life ass niggas. My momma made me feel like the scum of the earth when she found out I was gay. Now she laid up in the hospital because she overdosed on drugs."

I told Lump all about how I got caught sucking dick and how my mother reacted to me when I got home.

He wasn't surprised at all because his mother acts the same way towards him now.

"LD my mother is really delusional. I don't know what type of drugs she's on but she seriously needs help. She blames me for breaking up our *family!* She told me that if it weren't for my gay ass, her man wouldn't be behind bars right now. I couldn't even say anything to her. I just felt sorry that she even felt that way. I can't change who she is, and I have no choice but to love her either way because she's my mother."

I told him about me not wanting to go see my mother in the hospital, and he made me promise that I would go see her.

"LD you only get one mother. You don't get to choose your parents so you're stuck with whatever you're born into. You don't want anything to happen to her in there. You will have to live with that for the rest of your life if she doesn't make it out alive. She was on drugs, so you know everything she said to you was because of that. After everything my mother has put me through, I would still visit her in the hospital if something happened to her. You should really go visit her, even if its only once."

I thought about what Lump had said and Tony pretty much told me the same thing. If Lump went through all that he went through with his mother and would still go visit her, then I guess I could too. I was going to wait until I got paid at the end of the week. I needed all of my money I had for bus fare to get to work for the next few days.

Lump and I continued talking and laughing for the next few hours. He kept me laughing so hard that my side was hurting. I never thought in a million years that I would have a punk friend, but Lump was pretty cool with me. I guess I just didn't want to be classified as gay and that's why I tried to stay away from him. Now that I started becoming more and more comfortable with my sexuality, I was ok with being his friend. I guess deep down, Lump was everything I couldn't be at the time – out and proud.

Tony called me about an hour after Lump had left. He asked me all about my night. He knew I was going to the gay club for the first time and was interested to hear how it was. I told him all about it and how Lump had came over today and we actually had a decent conversation. It was too early to tell but Lump and I may end up being really good friends. Tony seemed happy that I was able to find a gay homeboy that I could actually relate to. Tony just listened to me as I told him some of the stuff lump and I had discussed earlier. I kept asking Tony if he was ok with our conversation cause I didn't want him to feel uncomfortable at all. He said he was fine and would let me know if it became too much for him to listen to.

I was glad Tony had called me. I loved talking to him on the phone. We stayed on the phone for hours and it never got quiet. He told me all about growing up with foster parents and being thankful that he had them in his life. He said he was too young to remember that he was even adopted. His foster parents told him on his eighteenth birthday. He told me that they didn't mind him wanting to know who his real parents were and wouldn't object to him looking for them. Tony was curious to know who they were and why they gave him up, but didn't want to go through the hassle of looking for them. I couldn't argue with him about that. I wouldn't want to spend my time looking for two people that obviously didn't want me either. I just listened to him though.

We ended up talking until two in the morning before we decided to go to sleep. We told each other good night and we hung up. I realized that I was smiling after I hung up the phone. I really enjoyed talking to Tony everyday. He obviously enjoyed it too because we were on the phone for hours at a time. I wondered where his girlfriend was because she didn't interrupt our call this time. I wasn't really concerned about her at all, just a little curious.

Chapter 11

I woke up the next day to someone beating on my door around 8 a.m. I ran to the door to see who the fuck was beating on it like they were the police. I opened the door and it was Boo. He was smiling from ear to ear.

"Damn bro, I thought you were the police."

"Happy B-Day my nigga!"

Damn I had forgot my birthday was today. I had finally turned sixteen years old and didn't even realize it. I had been on the phone all night with Tony and completely forgot about my big day. Well hell, at least I was on the phone with Tony when the clock struck twelve. I had brought in my birthday with Tony and I was oblivious to the fact.

"Thanks Boo, I had almost forgot it was my birthday."

"You're welcome bro! I got a big surprise for you too!"

Before I could even ask what it was, Mike stepped through the door and I damn near passed out. I hugged him so hard and I almost started crying. Mike was sexier than ever. He had clearly been eating good in jail because he had gotten taller and way more muscular than he had ever been. He looked so fucking good to me. I wanted to pull his dick out and suck it right there in front of Boo.

"Welcome home Mike! Damn I missed you bro!"

"Thanks LD, I missed you too. I'm happy to be home."

Boo took off to go catch his school bus. He would have stayed home today but they had to take pictures for the football team, and he couldn't miss that. Mike came inside and we talked for a while. I caught him up on everything that had been happening in the hood since he's been gone. He told me some things that had happened around here that I didn't even know about. I wondered how he knew what was happening in the streets of Dallas and he was locked up two hundred miles away. Then he dropped the bomb on me and told me that his baby momma was letting him know everything.

I was shocked to hear he even had a baby momma. No one mentioned anything to me about a baby before this. Mike told me that this girl named Shaun had gotten pregnant right before he got locked up and she said it was his. He didn't want anyone to know until he got out and could get a DNA test on the little boy. I told him that was smart of him because these hoes around here will blame a baby on anybody. If you even kiss they ass the wrong way they'll swear they pregnant! He wanted to get the DNA test as soon as possible so he could take care of his son - if he was really his.

We talked for an hour before I finally turned the tables on him.

"What's up with that dick Mike?"

"What you mean?"

"It's been too long since I sucked yo' dick and I think its about time."

Mike just looked at me and smiled, "Nigga don't just talk about it, come eat this dick up then!" I walked over to Mike and got on my knees. His dick was already rock hard when I pulled it out of his sweats. I looked at it and my mouth got extra wet. I had been waiting four years to finally suck his big ass dick, and now I had my chance. I stuck his dick in my mouth and sucked and slurped all over it. I licked from his balls all the way up to the tip of his dick and sucked on his head some more. He just leaned back on the couch and had his eyes closed with his mouth wide open. He was moaning the whole time. He finally started moaning louder and louder until his dick exploded a fresh batch of nut deep into my mouth. I swallowed every drop too. Mike just sat there on the couch for a while. He said he couldn't move. I had sucked every ounce of energy he had out of him.

I was beyond excited about sucking Mike's dick. After all these years I had finally had the opportunity to redeem myself and it was better than I had hoped it would be. I got Mike a towel so that he could wash his dick off. Mike lifted up his t-shirt and I noticed that he was tatted up.

"When did you get those tats?"

"My homeboy did all these while I was locked up."

I was confused.

"You can get tattoos in prison? How do they get needles and stuff to do them?"

"They make all that shit in there, or they sneak it in. It's a way to get whatever you want inside there."

"Wow! How do they clean that shit cause I wouldn't think it's sanitary to do that in there."

"Shit I don't know about all that bro. Everybody was gettin' these hoes so I got some too."

He washed up and asked me where the lotion was.

"What you need lotion for?"

"So I can get in that ass now."

I was confused. "Huh? You want to fuck me?"

"Yea, don't you want me to?"

"Oh naw, I don't think I'm ready for all that yet."

"Oh, you aint never been fucked before?"

"Naw, I only suck dick for now."

"Damn You aint never been fucked? I bet yo pussy tighter than a motherfucka' then! I would love to break you in!"

Pussy? Is that what straight niggas referred to our ass-holes as…pussy? I needed to ask Lump what that was all about. I looked at Mike's dick and he was on hard again. His dick was entirely too big to be shoving up my asshole anytime soon. I did want to get fucked one day but my first time wasn't going to be with a big ass dick like Mike had!

"You fucked around while you was locked up?"

"Hell yea I did. Shit I was in there for four years. I was getting pussy thrown at me everyday out here in the free world. You think I can just stop fucking one day - cold turkey? It was entirely too much ass walking around that prison for me not to fuck around. I'm tired of people asking me that stupid shit though. I will never admit it, I tell them naw I didn't do no bullshit like that. I'll tell them I had a homeboy that was fuckin' around in there wit' them niggas though. They seem to believe that shit so I use that everytime."

Damn I had never thought about that. It never crossed my mind that Mike was locked up with all them niggas everyday, and they had to do what they had to do in order to survive. It's only so much jacking off that a nigga could do before he went insane. I guess if niggas is all you have to choose from then you have to adapt. Shit niggas do it in the free world everyday, how could I be so dumb as to not realize he was in there fucking around?

"Man we fucked around whenever we needed a nut. Nobody said shit about it though. What goes on behind bars, stay behind bars. Niggas that have been locked up before understand the code. You do what you have to in order to survive in there."

I understood the code too. I never told anyone anything about the niggas I had sucked up and I had never even been locked up before. I respected their privacy and I wasn't going to risk losing my trade over someone finding out about us. Mike wished me a happy birthday again on the way out the door and he told me that he would be hitting me up for some more later on. I laughed and locked the front door after he left.

~ ~ ~ ~

The next few days went by really fast. I had gone back to school and everything was pretty calm. Jay and I were still cool, and he still sat next to me in our science class. He whispered to me during class that he wanted to finish what we started real soon. I gave him my cell phone number and told him to just let me know whenever he was ready. I had also seen Chris for he first time since we beat the shit out of him, but he walked past me like he didn't even see me.

Lump and I would talk in the hallways all the time and occasionally over the phone. We had started getting closer and closer. She was starting to become a really good friend. Lump kept me laughing and we would always seem to end up in the same place everyday looking at the different niggas that walked by. He told me that he had actually had sex with more people in our school than I had originally thought. That didn't surprise me though. These niggas around here were willing to fuck anything with a hole.

Tony and I had been talking every day. We took our breaks together at work and would sit on the phone at night for hours talking and laughing. I started getting use to our phone conversations and didn't want them to end anytime soon. It was already payday and I was going to receive my first paycheck. He had talked me into going to visit my mom after work. I kept putting it off and now that I finally had some money in my pockets, I could ride the train there and make it back home.

I was scheduled to get off at 7:00 p.m. so I figured today was the perfect day for a visit. My mom had the doctor call and ask me to bring her some clothes. I told him I would come today with a few items for her. My mother hadn't called the house at all since she started her treatment. I was kind of glad she didn't call either. Between school, work, and talking to Lump and Tony on the phone, I just didn't have time to deal with her and all her drama.

I had cashed my check and left work for the day. Tony had taken his break and walked me to the train station. He told me that he was proud of me for going to see my mom. As the train was pulling up, he grabbed me around my waist and hugged me. I was shocked. We had never been that close before! I reached up and wrapped my arms around his neck and hugged him back. He told me that he would call me when he got off and to make sure my phone was charged up.

I got on the train smiling from ear to ear. I actually liked Tony. I had never felt this way about a guy before in my life. I never wanted anything more than dick from all the other guys, but it was something different about

Tony. It was like we had a connection and I was falling for him more and more each day. He had to have felt the same way too. I don't know many straight guys that are going to hug on me the way that he did and think that's ok. I couldn't wait to talk to him on the phone to see what that hug was all about.

The train let me off a block away from the hospital. I started walking in the direction of the hospital when two men came out of an alley. They were walking behind me and I couldn't help but get nervous. I wanted to speed up a little but I decided to just take it slow. Before I could make it to the corner they grabbed me and one of them put his hand over my mouth so I couldn't scream. I kicked and fought but they were too big. They drug me into an alley and went through my pants pocket. I heard one of them shout, "Jackpot" after he found my money I had just received from my paycheck. They threw me to the ground and ran off.

I sat there on the ground dazed and confused. I had just been robbed for my entire paycheck. Everything I worked hard for that entire week was taken from me in the blink of an eye. As I sat there, I started to get angrier and angrier. I was so mad that I started crying uncontrollably. I was extremely pissed. I wanted to blame everyone else for what happened. First I blamed my mother for being in the hospital in the first place. Then I blamed Tony and Lump for encouraging me to go see her. If it hadn't been for them, I wouldn't have been put in this situation.

I pulled myself together and realized I still had my mother's bag of clothes in my hand. I took the bag of clothes and chunked it so far down the alley that I thought I would never hear the bag hit the ground. I was pissed that I was robbed trying to come see her fat ass. I lost all my money because she was a fucking dope fiend. I was mad at anybody and everybody. All I wanted to do was get home and shower so I could go to sleep.

After I got out of the shower I looked at my cell phone and saw that I had two missed calls from Tony. I sat my phone down and got in the bed. I didn't want to talk to anyone. Just as I was about to lay down, the phone started ringing again. It was Tony.

"Hello!"

"Wassup LD? I've been calling you trying to see how things went at the hospital."

"I didn't make it to the fuckin' hospital!"

"Why not? I thought we had a deal?"

"I got robbed for my whole check right outside of the fuckin' hospital that's why!"

"What! You got robbed on the way to the hospital and they took your whole check?"

"You heard me the first time nigga! It's all your fault too!"

"Huh? How is it all my fault? LD I care about you too much to put you in that type of danger!"

"Nigga care about these fuckin' nuts!"

-Click!

I hung up my phone in his face. He called back four times back to back before I finally shut the power off on my cell phone.

I woke up in a better mood the next day. I realized that it wasn't anyone's fault that I had been robbed. No one would have known that some low life ass thugs were lurking in an alley waiting for me to walk by so they could take all my money. I couldn't blame anyone for that and I finally realized that once I had time to calm down.

School and work went by pretty quick that day. Tony was off so I didn't get a chance to see him. I was hoping he would call me so that I could apologize for the way I acted towards him. I was home watching TV when my cell phone started ringing. I was hoping it was Tony calling, but I didn't recognize the number on the caller ID, so I knew it wasn't him.

"Hello?"

As soon as I heard that sexy, deep, manly voice on the other end, I knew exactly who it was.

"Say my nigga, wassup? What you doin' right now?"

"Nothin' major, I'm just watching TV."

"Well shit come over here and hook me up."

"I'm on my way."

It was Mike. He wanted some more head. I was glad he did cause I needed something to cheer me up. Pleasing Mike always made me feel better and today was the perfect day for that. I didn't hesitate whenever he called. I walked out the door and was headed to Mike's house when my phone rang again. Mike was calling me back.

"Hello?"

"I forgot to tell you that I'm not at home. I'm at Shaun's' house."

"What? So you want me to come to yo' baby momma house and suck yo' dick?"

"Yea and hurry up. She went to the store so we gotta make this quick!"

"Why didn't you just come over here to my crib?"

"Cause I got my lil nigga here with me. He playin' around wit his toys though so we good."

I was completely speechless. This wasn't the same Mike I had known all these years. This nigga went to jail for four years and came out a totally different person. This nigga was laid up in his *alleged* baby momma house and while he was supposed to be bonding with his *alleged* son, he wanted me to come over there to suck his dick. Shaun had gone to the store to get them something to eat, and he wanted me to sneak in her house before she returned to suck his dick. None of this really surprised me, because I had done the same thing with plenty of niggas in our complex. Maybe if I didn't give a fuck about Mike, this situation would have been a lot different. However, this time I was disgusted with what he wanted me to do. I knew Mike was better than that, and he was only going to get worse if I enabled his sexual greed this time.

I said, "Sorry Mike, I just can't do this." I hung up the phone and went back into my house. I was really trying to figure out what was going through Mike's head. He called me so that I could rush over to his girl house to suck his dick while she was at the store. He was looking after a four-year-old little boy, but wanted to distract him with toys while he got his dick sucked by another nigga. Mike had taken a turn for the worst and I didn't want to be involved in any of that. He had some good dick, a nice body, and could talk anyone into anything. Hell, he could probably sell pussy to a prostitute! I knew all of that was a recipe for disaster though, and he was on a path to destruction.

By the time I got out of the shower I still hadn't received a call from Tony. I was a little worried so I decided to call him first.

"Hello?"

"Hey Tony! Wassup wit' you?"

"Oh you wanna talk now huh? You done throwing your little bitch fit?"

"I'm sorry Tony. I really was pissed off yesterday and I took it out on anybody I could. I didn't mean any of it. It was just my anger talking. Will you forgive me?"

Tony was quiet for a while.

"I don't know if I can do that."

We both laughed. Tony was always joking around and it made me feel special. We talked about everything that happened with the robbery and he was really mad that I had to go through that.

"You want to chill after work Friday? There is a movie that I wanna' see."

"Nigga you know I aint got no money, so I don't even know why you playin' wit' me like that."

"I know that. I wouldn't ask you out if I wasn't going to pay for you. That's what real niggas do. Im sure your use to those project niggas that ask you for money huh?"

I laughed at Tony, "Nigga shut up!"

Damn he wants me to go on a date with him and he's going to pay my way?

"Yea I'll go wit you, I guess."

"Good we need to start doing stuff more often since we're taking this to the next level."

Hold up, did this nigga just say we taking this to the next level? My heart started beating faster.

"What do you mean Tony?"

"I like you LD. I aint never been around a gay dude before and I'm starting to like you. At first I thought that if you were a girl you would be perfect for me. Then I started to realize that you are better than a girl for me. You're like the best of both worlds. We can kick it and have fun like we boys, but still have sex if we wanted to. I aint never had sex wit a guy, but I can't say what I won't do in the future. I really think I'm starting to fall for you. I think we should try being in a relationship."

I had never thought about being in a relationship before. I didn't even know what I was supposed to do in one. I had never been in a situation where a relation-ship was even a possibility. All the niggas around here wanted was a nut. They weren't trying to establish any-thing with anyone. They wanted to roam the streets and fuck as much as they could. That's what I assumed was normal behavior, until Tony came along.

"I think we should be in a relationship too Tony. I really like you and I enjoy our conversations. It's some-thing different about you. You aint like all these other niggas out here, and I don't want to lose you."

"So I guess we go together now?"

I smiled, "Yea, I guess we do."

Tony and I talked for the rest of the night. We talked and laughed until his battery finally died on his phone. I went to sleep on cloud nine. I couldn't believe that I had a boyfriend. Not only did I have a boyfriend, but he was also smart, so fucking sexy, and had a great sense of humor. I couldn't ask for a better man than that.

Chapter 12

Our relationship was going great. We had gone to the movies a few times and also out to eat. We were together everyday after work. He would walk me to the train station at night and hug and kiss me in front of everybody that would be standing out there. He didn't seem to care, so I didn't mind either. Of course we got some crazy stares and a few laughs, but we were in our own world. We hadn't actually had sex yet, but the love and affection that he showed me was better than having sex. He did want to have sex with me eventually, but we wanted it to be special so we decided to wait. I already knew I was going to let him be the first guy to fuck me. From what I had been grabbing on through his pants, I could tell it wasn't going to be an easy task for me.

I came home from school one day and found my mother sitting on the couch. I smelled weed, so I knew she was up to her old tricks. *Damn she just got out and couldn't wait to roll up a blunt!* It hadn't been sixty days yet, so I knew she couldn't have been back on the right track.

"So you just gon' walk up in my motherfuckin' house and don't speak?"

I rolled my eyes at her. *Here we go with this shit again!*

"I sat up there in that motherfuckin' hospital for damn near a month, and yo' bitch ass didn't even come see me. The doctor told me that he asked you to bring me some clothes, and yo' ass still didn't come! I'm done wit yo' faggot ass! If you think you gon' continue to disrespect me while you walk around my house all day suckin' dicks and gettin' fucked in the ass, you got another motherfuckin' thang comin'! I'm bout to look for all my other kids 'cause you are a big fuckin' disappointment to me. I'm tryna get my life together and you aint doing shit but stressing me the fuck out. I should throw you out right on yo' faggot ass!"

I had reached my boiling point with my mother. It had taken everything in me not to punch her in her fucking face. She had pushed every button I had, and I blew up before I knew it.

"Fuck you fat ass dope fiend bitch! You not gon' keep talking to me like that!"

She just sat there with a surprised ass look on her face. I walked to my room and slammed my door. I locked it cause I knew it wouldn't be long before she was trying to barge in to kick my ass. As soon as I sat on my bed she started beating on my room door. She was cursing and yelling at me through the door. I didn't care what she was saying though. She was the one on the other side looking like a fool. I started cleaning up my room while trying to ignore her. I ran across the card that the Navy recruiter had left on my door. I stuck it inside my drawer just incase I ever needed it. I wasn't going to let her ruin my day. I got dressed and left for work. When I walked through the living room she was smoking a blunt and looking through the phone book. She looked at me and said, "Oh yo' faggot ass got a job now? Well you better have my motherfuckin' rent money on the 1st!" I had to stop and look at her. "You don't even pay rent so shut the fuck up you fat ass bitch!" The next thing I knew the phone book flew by my face almost hitting me. I just shook my head at her as I walked out the door.

After work, Tony invited me to come his house because his parents had gone out of town for the weekend. I was glad we had a chance to be alone and spend some quality time with each other. We had a chance to talk about everything that had happened between my mother and I.

From the way his house looked, I assumed that his parents had a lot of money. He lived in a two-story house in a very nice neighborhood. They had nice furniture and the house was clean from top to bottom. They had antique furniture in the living room and a pool built in the back yard. It was the biggest house I had ever been in. He led me upstairs to his bedroom after I finished looking around.

We were in his room kissing and laying in his bed. He turned me on my stomach then got on top of me and started grinding on my ass. He was kissing on my neck and he was starting to make me horny. He whispered in my ear, "You want this dick don't you?" I whispered back to him, "Yea daddy, I want it." Honestly, I did want his dick. I didn't know if he was talking about fucking me or just getting head. I could tell by the way he was pressing that dick against my ass that getting head wasn't exactly what he wanted from me. I was nervous though. I had never let anyone do that to me. I remembered everything Lump had told me and I was going to try it out just to see if it would work.

Tony turned out the lights and pulled his clothes off. I pulled mine off too and laid on his bed. He got some baby oil out of his drawer and sat it on the bed. I was lying on my back and he got on top of me. He was kissing me all over my body while he was grinding on me. He stood next to the bed and told me to suck his dick. He knew I liked to be talked dirty to. I just love it when a nigga tells me what to do when I'm sucking him. He moaned as he began to thrust his big dick in and out of my mouth. He would go deep down to the back of my throat and pull it all the way out until the tip of his dick was resting on my lips. He moaned loudly and I did too. He loved every minute of it, and so did I.

He laid me on my stomach and squirted baby oil all over my ass. He rubbed it on my ass cheeks as he started to kiss them. He spread my ass cheeks apart and stuck his tongue in my ass hole. He was eating me out and I couldn't do anything but moan. I had never experienced that before and the feeling was the best in the world. I was moaning and squirming up the bed as he chowed down on my ass. I couldn't believe how good it felt. *If I had known it felt like this I would have given up this ass a long time ago!* He kissed each ass cheek as he put some baby oil on his dick. He kissed me on the back of my neck as he said, "You ready to feel this dick in you?" I just moaned and told him, "Yea daddy, this ass is all yours."

He gently eased the tip of his dick inside me. He wasn't forcing it inside, but it still hurt and I moaned in pain. He eased up a little and just kept kissing me and fingering my hole. He tried to stick it in again and I decided to just take the pain like a man this time. He eased inside of me and just let his dick rest for a minute. Pretty soon I relaxed and I felt my muscles in my ass hole open up. He started to slide in and out of me. I moaned and he moaned. He was really inside of me and it felt so good. He kissed me and fucked me at the same time. He started going faster and faster as we both moaned louder and louder. It seemed as though the louder he got, the louder I would get. I guess it was too tight for him to continue any longer. A minute after he had finally entered my virgin ass hole, he nutted all over my cheeks. He was satisfied with this stress relief he had experienced for the first time, and so was I. He laid on top of me as he held me in his arms, and it felt great.

He was out of breath as he whispered in my ear, "Damn that felt better than pussy! I love you baby." I didn't know what pussy felt like, and I really didn't give a fuck. All I was concerned with was the fact that I wasn't a virgin anymore, and I had been fucked by the only nigga that ever really loved me. I whispered back to him, "I love you too daddy." I laid in his arms until we both fell asleep.

~ ~ ~ ~

Life was going great for me. I had finished the school year and was now working full time at the store over the summer. My checks were coming in regularly and I was able to save most of them. The only thing I had to pay for was bus fare or the occasional hotel room with Tony. We had started making love more often and we couldn't be any happier with each other. He would pay for everything the majority of the times we went on dates, and I would take care of it if he couldn't. We were in love and we were extremely happy with each other.

My mother and I weren't speaking at all. I didn't say shit to her, and she didn't say shit to me. I was fine with that. One day she was in the living room on the phone trying to sound all proper and I overheard her tell someone that she loved all her kids and she would just like to contact them to see how they're doing. I let out the loudest, "Ha!" I could possibly come up with. She just threw the middle finger up at me and I laughed as I left out the door.

Boo and I were sitting outside on the steps one day when Lump walked up. He hugged me and said, "Hey bitch!" I laughed and spoke back to him. Boo spoke to Lump also. Boo sat there for a minute as me and Lump talked. Then he got up and started to walk off. I stopped talking to Lump and asked Boo where he was going. He smiled at us and said, "I'll leave you two ladies alone so y'all can gossip." Lump and I laughed as Boo turned and walked off.

Lump couldn't wait for Boo to walk off. He had a look in his eyes like he had sum juicy gossip and I was ready to hear it.

"Bitch I aint gon' tell you how trade fucked me down last night!"

"Unh Unh! Po' me the tea bitch!" I was able to use my gay lingo around Lump and not feel weird. We talked like that to each other everyday and it was like second nature for us. I wouldn't dare talk like that around Tony though. He called it "punk talk." Tony would look at me and laugh so hard if I used those words around him.

"Well bitch, last night I was walking the streets tryin' to pick up trade when a nigga came out of the trap. I couldn't see his face but I knew he was following me and I led him to the field over there that leads to the rec' center. Well when I turned around I noticed that it was Boo's brother that just got out the pen a few months ago!"

My heart started beating so fast. I already knew Mike was out there bad, but now he was picking up niggas off the street! I just stood there with my mouth wide open as Lump talked.

"Chile he told me to hurry up and bend over cause he gotta get back to the crib before his baby momma started looking for him. I pulled out my lube and gave him a condom. I bent over and he went to work on me. He tore my poor little booty hole up chile! He busted his nut and just walked off before I even had a chance to get myself together honey! When I pulled up my shorts, I turned around and saw my lube and the condom on the ground. He didn't even open the condom I gave him and that hoe ass nigga nutted in me! Chile I know you got a nigga and y'all be all boo'd up and shit, but be careful cause the trade out here these days are a mess. I haven't even finished all my medication and he gon' just fuck me raw like that. Then he got the nerve to nut in me again!"

I was confused, "What medication? And what you mean *again*?"

"Bitch he fucked me about a month ago inside that hoe Shaun house while she was gone to the doctor. He said he needed to bust a nut real bad cause her pussy was garbage. He fucked me raw and nutted in me that time too. About a week later I was itching real bad inside my ass hole and it turned out that nigga gave me Chlamydia. I saw him walking one day and I told him what he did to me. He told me to go get my pills that the doctor prescribed me so he could see how they look. Well bitch when I came back, he took 'em from me! He told me to tell my doctor that I had lost them and to give me some more cause he was keeping those for himself! Bitch I just stood there in shock and he walked off with my pills!"

"Hell naw Lump! And you fucked him again last night?"

"Bitch don't act all Mother Theresa on me hoe! I was horny, and chile he got some good ass dick!"

We both laughed. I found it more disturbing than funny though. I knew a while back that Mike was on a path to destruction, but this confirmed it. He was a sex addict and he was addicted to niggas ass holes while pretending to be straight. I'm sure Shaun didn't have a clue what he was doing when she wasn't around either. I didn't have anything to say that would make the situation any better, so I just looked at the ground and shook my head as lump went on.

My mother and I still hadn't been talking to each other. The only time she did say something to me was when the Navy recruiter stopped by to check on me. She had the nerve to stand there in front of him and pretend to be one of those loving and caring mothers. I laughed so hard on the inside. She told him that she wants all her kids to do better than she did and to get out of the hood by any means necessary. I just rolled my eyes at her as she went on. I told him that I would be in touch if I did decide that the Navy was right for me.

He told me that he would check on me occasionally to see how I was doing and to let him know if I was ready to sign up at any time.

I was at work one day and Tony kept calling my phone back to back. I couldn't answer cause I was on the register. It was the first of the month and the store was packed. We were short on cashiers because two people had called in sick. I finally got a break and I went to the break room to call him back. He didn't even answer his phone. I was sitting there drinking my juice when they called me back up to the front over the intercom system. I already knew the lines were backed up again because that's the only time they would call me back early. I was walking to the front when I felt my phone vibrating and saw that it was Tony. I answered the call as I hurried to the front of the store. "Wassup baby?" I could tell by his voice that he was excited. "Baby I got some great news!" By the time he said that, I had reached the front of store and needed to jump back on my register cause the lines were ridiculous.

"Baby we are really packed today so Ima' call you as soon as I get off in two hours so you can tell me all about it."

"Baby I'm bout to meet…"

I didn't give him a chance to respond. I hung up the phone and started checking out customers.

The last two hours of work went by quickly. It always seemed to go by fast when the store was packed for some reason. I turned in my cash drawer and headed home.

I was on my way home and I had called Tony five times but he still didn't answer. I wanted to know what he was so happy about. He had been calling me all morning and now when I could talk to him, he wouldn't answer for me. I wanted to be excited with him, but I couldn't listen to his news while I was at work. I knew he would understand though. He knew how crazy the 1st of the month was for us.

I walked into the house and it smelled unusually good. It was like fresh Lysol or something. It appeared as though my mother had cleaned up. When I walked in, my mother jumped up off the couch. There was an older black couple sitting in the living room and my mother introduced them as Mr. and Mrs. Williams. I spoke to them and went to my room. My mother followed me. She came in and closed the door behind her. She walked up to me and grabbed me by the front of my shirt. She clinched her teeth and said, "You little faggot ass bitch, if you fuck this up for me I will beat the shit outta' you! I found my other son and he's in the bathroom. You come out here and introduce yourself and you better talk like a fuckin' man! I told you I wasn't raising no mothafuckin' faggots up in here so I went out and found my other kids. He's a real nigga too, so you should try to be more like him instead of suckin' dick and shit! Now get yo' ass out here and introduce yo' self!"

My first mind told me to sock her fat ass in the mouth, but I knew that would be a big mistake. I did have about three thousand dollars saved up, but that wouldn't last me very long out on the streets. I just looked at her as she walked out of my room. I had wanted to meet my older brothers and sisters for a while. I wanted to see if they came out better because they were taken away from our mother at a young age and didn't have to endure all of the bullshit she had to offer.

My mother was standing in the living room as I walked up. I could tell someone was standing in front of her but I couldn't see them because I was still in the hallway. She looked at me and said, "La'Darious I would like you to meet your brother, Antonio." I turned the corner and looked at his face. Our eyes locked and we both just looked at each other in shock. I was staring into the eyes of my older brother, my mothers' third child, my sibling, my coworker, my first love…my Tony. We didn't get a chance to say anything to each other. The only thing I can remember after seeing his face is every drop of blood in my body rushing to my head. My heart started beating faster and faster right before my knees gave out and I passed out on the living room floor.

The following is an excerpt from an upcoming book:

The Slurpee Chronicles: If These Cheeks Could Talk

I honestly believe that sex runs the world. We wouldn't even be here today without it. Sex has many different faces. It really can be a beautiful thing if it's done with the right person. On the other hand, it can also be a nightmare. Sometimes you can run across someone like me that will fool you. I'm the type that can make the sex seem as though it's a beautiful thing at first, but then it turns out to be a nightmare in disguise.

My name is Tatiana Monroe, but my birth name was Tyson Moore. Most of the niggas around here don't care that I have a dick between my legs. As long as I look like a female and let them feel on my fat ass and big titties, they will stick they dicks in any hole on me that will make them bust a nut. You have to understand that these niggas are "straight" too. They have girlfriends, wives, and families and shit like that. All of that has nothing to do with me though. I don't care what they got waiting on them at home. These women need to understand that what they won't do, I damn sure will! My job is to provide a service that they obviously aint getting at home.

When these niggas come to me, they expect to bust a good ass nut wherever they want and then leave-with no strings attached of course. Most of the time they don't even use a condom when they fuck me. I don't make them use one either. Hell, I'm already HIV positive so they aint fucking up my life. They taking that shit back home to they wives, girlfriends, or baby mommas. I don't give a fuck about none of that. Shit if they letting these down low ass niggas fuck them raw, then that's on them. I make no apologies for what I do. Hell the streets gave it to me, so I'm just giving it right back.

Made in the USA
Charleston, SC
20 July 2015